KANE

ALEXANDER SHIFTER BROTHERS
BOOK ONE

SELINA COFFEY

LOVY BOOKS

Lovy Books Ltd
20-22 Wenlock Road
London N1 7GU
United Kingdom

Cover by SC Creative

"Damesha, please, I can't keep a dog in my apartment. You're allowed pets," the voice on the phone pleaded.

Damesha Parker sighed, staring down at her smartphone where her best friend Erika's voice floated from. She absolutely did not need this today. Her best friend had found a Beagle wandering the street and now she wanted Damesha to take care of her. That was just like Erika, saving the world through other people's graces.

She finally had to laugh and agreed, telling her friend to bring the dog over before she hung up the phone. Erika might be saving the world, but Damesha was going to be saving this dog.

"What am I going to do with a dog? Sheesh!" she said, pulling her soft blue sweater around her as she sat back down. Just as she did, she heard a knock on the door. Getting right back up, she peered through the security hole to make sure it was Erika. This was New York City after all; you didn't just assume you knew who it was and open the door to whoever could be out there.

She opened the door with a laugh as a streak of red and white ran past her, straight into her living room. Erika quickly walked into the room, a short woman with long blond hair and skin so pale her dark brown eyes seemed to be swimming on their own. She was beautiful, but in an unconventional way. Her pale appearance gave her an angelic look that could be deceiving as Erika was a fiercely loyal friend and advocate for all kinds of causes.

"Seriously, Damesha, this dog is going to be so good for you!" Erika hugged her much darker friend and stared up into the woman's blue eyes, her own brown ones shining happily.

"Girl, I'm leaving in a week, what am I going to do with a dog? A dog of all things?" Damesha went into the kitchen to prepare the usual cup of hot tea that Erika asked for when offered. She passed a mirror on the way and saw what people usually saw, a dark-skinned African-American woman, tall, with a fine bone structure, high cheekbones, and almond-shaped eyes that many said reminded them of statues of Cleopatra.

It was her startling light blue eyes that usually caught people's attention, many staring and gasping when they saw the color. At twenty-eight years old Damesha still could not get used to the attention, though she'd learned to endure the questions people felt obliged to ask upon meeting her.

Damesha heard the tap of toenails behind her and looked down as something soft pushed against her leg. Kneeling down, she patted the dog.

"You're so little but somehow so big, aren't you?" Damesha smiled at the dog who seemed to smile back. She was petting the dog under the chin, looking her over for injuries or problem areas when the dog hunkered down and skittered away at the sound of an unfamiliar noise.

Damesha stood up quickly and turned the kettle off. The whistle of the kettle on the stove had scared the poor dog. Damesha knelt back down, her lithe frame bending down to her knees easily, to comfort the startled dog.

"Awwww! It's okay baby, it's just the kettle." The dog looked up at Damesha with frightened but trusting eyes. Damesha held her hand out once more and the dog walked to her with an uncertain expression. "You poor love. Imagine what your life has been like! Let me see what we can feed you."

Damesha made the tea and found a leftover hunk of beef roast she'd been planning to heat up for dinner. She shred the beef into a bowl and put it down for the now quivering dog. Damesha was amazed as the dog ate carrots and potatoes as well as the meat.

"You were hungry!" The dog looked up at Damesha with a happy smile, her whole body waving as her tail wagged happily. "Alright, you can stay."

Damesha heard a cheer from the living room and went through, carrying two cups of tea.

"If this dog eats my entire house, I'm blaming you. Now, what are we going to name her?" Damesha laughed once more as the dog jumped into her lap, settling into a position that let Damesha know she was guarding. She stroked the dog's head, smoothing down her head, loving the silky feel of the dog's fur.

"Rover?" Erika offered with a laugh.

"No, I hate names like that. We need a real name. Hmm." She tapped her lip and watched as the dog jumped down, sniffing around the apartment, getting her bearings.

"Orphan Annie?" Erika said suddenly, her expression one of sudden enlightenment. "She's on her own, she's got red fur, well some of it's red, and she's been saved by a benevolent caretaker!"

"Hmm. I really don't know about the orphan part but

Annie might work. Annie?" Damesha called out to the curious critter now inspecting a carpet as though it was a deadly beast about to snap and bite her snout. The dog looked up when Damesha called out and came back to the woman that smelled like love and friendship.

"Do you like that name? Are you an Annie?" Damesha laughed as the dog propped herself on Damesha's legging covered knees and swiped a long tongue across her cheek. "Annie it is then. Girl, I hope you like to travel!"

Annie's response was a wiggling body and more puppy kisses as Erika and Damesha loved on her. This wasn't how Damesha was planning to spend her final weekend in the city but you did what you had to for friends. Besides, she'd known Annie was coming, she'd dreamed about her the night before. Damesha didn't try to talk with people about it anymore but she was a little bit psychic.

As a child, she'd tried to talk to her elders about it, warn them about some of the things she'd seen in her dreams, but her grandmother had quickly hushed her, telling her to keep such things to herself. Damesha hadn't understood exactly why she was supposed to keep quiet, but after years of getting into trouble for warning people about things that were going to happen, she'd learned to keep her mouth shut. It was bad enough being stared at because of her eyes. Making people think she was crazy didn't help.

The power had started to dim over time, instead of getting flashes of the future when she touched someone or from her dreams, things had kind of settled down to a low hum of feeling something but not always being sure what. Kind of like when you have a vivid dream but can't remember it five minutes after waking up. Sometimes she could hear people's thoughts, a gross invasion she tried to avoid because it just made her feel dirty, but trying to block it didn't always work out the way she wanted it to. Sometimes she heard things, things she didn't want to hear, and there just wasn't much she could do to stop it.

DAMESHA PUT Annie's lead on as she exited the car, amazed at how well-behaved the dog was. Annie, the most awesome dog ever, didn't even need to be potty trained. Damesha was certain the dog hadn't grown up on the streets but had been abandoned there recently by some cruel owner. Annie had definitely been abused; she responded to every noise with fright, even paper rattling in the wind, but she was getting better.

Damesha hoped the staff in the restaurant would

come out to serve her. She'd been driving for days now and some places across the country weren't very accepting of dogs. Damesha hadn't seen many other places and none with tables outside. Damesha smiled as a pretty, petite waitress with gray eyes and black hair in a bun came out to take her order. Damesha ordered her food and poured a bottle of water into Annie's travel bowl.

It had been a whirlwind week but she'd managed to fit in a visit to the vet for Annie. Annie's shot had been updated, the vet confirmed that the "S" tattoo on Annie's belly meant she'd been spayed somewhere along the way, and gave her a clean bill of health. He also estimated Annie was around two years old by her teeth.

Damesha was keeping an eye on Annie, letting her explore under the table, when a cop drove by. Damesha rolled her eyes when he stopped suddenly and backed up, pulling in next to Damesha's little red economy sized car. Here we go.

Damesha braced herself as tall, overweight, and very sweaty older man got out of the police car and hitched up his khaki-colored pants before walking over to Damesha. She told herself maybe he just wanted to ask her a question about where she was from but she'd driven from New York to Kansas over the last few days.

This wasn't the first time a cop had felt a sudden urge to talk to her.

"Morning, little lady. What brings you to these parts?" the man asked from behind mirrored black sunglasses, his cowboy hat shading his face.

"I've come to do some research. I'm a writer." Damesha had learned long ago you keep your answer short and simple when the police talked to you. She sat at the table, without moving a muscle that wasn't vital to breathing, staring straight ahead.

"Right. A 'writer'. And what do you write about then, missy? Romance in the ghetto?" The disbelief and sarcasm in his gratingly high voice made Damesha go still with shock and anger.

She knew better than to take the bait, but she was about to retort when the waitress came back. Damesha held her tongue as the waitress set her food down and offered her condiments. It was probably for the best, Damesha really didn't want to get arrested so far from home.

"Leave it and be about your business," the policeman growled at the woman. Though his voice was high, something in his tone made the woman stop and stare at him.

The waitress scowled at him but did as she was told. Damesha picked through the pile of fries, wishing the man would just leave. Annie sat at her knee, looking up at her mistress with the hopes that a fry would fall from heaven for her.

"I guess you got some white in you somewhere or are those some kind of new contacts?" The man was rude, not just with his question but in his actions as he placed a foot on the bench beside Damesha and leaned over his knee. Staring down into her eyes, he turned his head several different ways, his eyes wrinkling at the sides as he squinted at her.

For her part, Damesha tried to avoid being so close to such bad breath. She slid further away from him, the vibes coming off of him making her physically sick. Something wasn't right with this man, not right at all, and that knowledge shook her deeply.

"One of my great grandmothers was Nordic," she responded politely as she took a bite of the burger she'd ordered, determined to show no fear. Even if she had to gag the burger down.

"Interesting. So how long are you going to be in town, little lady?" He was doing that classic cop-thing of rocking on his feet with his thumbs in his gun belt that always seemed to show up on classic cop shows. It was a pose meant to intimidate and remind the viewer the cop had a gun that he could use without qualm.

"That's enough, Pete, let the woman eat in peace. Go

on now. You have better things to do," a deep voice, gravelly and low, said from behind the man. The man walked into view and Damesha saw he was in his early thirties, and his handsome face was dark with anger. Obviously, he didn't like the way the policeman was treating her.

"I'm speaking to this here woman, Kane. Mind your own..." The man's face flushed when the taller man stepped up to the cop and his head dropped. "Yeah, I need to see what Marla needed."

"Tired of no account people coming into this town," the sheriff muttered but not to himself.

"That is more than enough, Pete," the man named Kane said. The sheriff stiffened. Kane's tone was made of steel, hard and cold. The policeman got in his car and drove away.

Damesha tried to keep her eyes from going round in wonder as she got a good look at the man the cop called Kane. Suddenly, Annie shot out from under the table where she'd been hiding and started licking at the handsome man's hand. He was tall, well over six foot, with black hair and tanned skin. He wore faded jeans with a well-worn black t-shirt and scuffed cowboy boots.

"Annie, stop that, it's rude!" Damesha pulled gently at Annie's lead but the dog was determined.

"It's fine and actually, Pete there was rude. I think

Annie's just saying hello." The man smiled down at Damesha and she saw his full rosy lips hid a set of straight white teeth. His voice was soft, though low, and a gentle air exuded from him. Beneath it all was tempered steel, but he was gentle with Damesha. She could feel herself relaxing already. Everything felt quiet around him. Peaceful.

"Would you like to sit with me? I could use a friendly face, and Annie seems to like you." The man knelt down to pet Annie and the two were happily getting to know each other. Annie pawed at his hands as they scratched her long floppy ears. Annie was in heaven.

"Ah, you're one of those that sees the sense of dogs. If a dog doesn't like someone right off the bat there's usually a good reason for it." The handsome dark-haired man gave Damesha a smile and she felt her heart bounce around in her chest.

"Annie's been a good judge so far. I trust her opinion. Have a seat, I don't think Annie's going to let you go now." She waved at a seat next to her and watched as Annie continued to lap up the attention happily.

Damesha noted as the man sat down that instead of the requisite cowboy hat the man had a ball cap in his back pocket. A fan of all genres of music, Damesha had noted in recent years that somewhere along the way country boys had gone from cowboy chic in Wrangler jeans and checked shirts to jeans that hugged their bottoms and tight black t-shirts. She thought of it as mechanic chic, a carefully studied air of not caring but making sure you showed off your assets.

Still, the man was well-spoken, polite, and had a breath-taking grin. It's what prompted her to invite him to sit with her, that gorgeous smile of his. She reminded herself she hadn't come to Kansas looking for love but to do research. Her gut told her to forget about it for a moment, this handsome fellow deserved a conversation. On top of that, her senses, her psychic buzz that some-times made being in crowds all but painful, was quiet at the moment, something that rarely happened. Damesha almost felt normal, whatever that meant.

"Do you often go around playing knight in shining, well black and denim, armor?" she teased as he took a seat on the bench across from her.

"Only when it's deserved. Pete's a bit of a douchebag, pardon me, but he is." Kane gave a rueful smile and laughed. "I think it's time for some new blood on the local police force. He thinks he owns the place."

"I'm sure he's just looking out for his people. Although, he really didn't need to be so rude or ask me about my eyes." Damesha had been looking into his black eyes, wondering why she was so drawn to this man that was so obviously used to being obeyed, even if his orders came softly. He was obviously an alpha male, and usually, that repulsed her. Something drew her to this man, though.

"They are beautiful eyes, though it's obvious how you got them, if I may say so," he responded with a low chuckle. "I bet you get asked about them often."

Damesha wished she'd worn more than a long t-shirt and her leggings as the man made her smile, but stopped worrying about it. He put her at ease. Somehow she knew this man was a defender, a kind man, though there was a glint of the rebel twinkling from those oddly dark eyes. And Annie loved him, she was between his legs, adoring him as he petted her, tongue lolling out happily as she blinked at Damesha in a "I know you're jealous" kind of way.

The waitress came and took Kane's order and they talked happily as Damesha ate. Kane insisted she finish her food before it went cold. She watched his hands as he stroked Annie, using his hands to punctuate his explanations. She liked how expressive he was. She also liked that they were so at ease with each other. They'd only just met but sitting with Kane was like sitting down with an old friend she hadn't seen in years.

Her eyes twinkled at him happily, and she began to respond to him, becoming at ease as she told him why she'd come to Kansas.

"I'm a writer, I write historical anthologies and biographies of little-known African-Americans throughout history. I'm here to research a former slave from Louisiana, a woman from the Civil War era. She came to Kansas after running away with a group of slaves because it was a free state." She stopped to take a sip of her iced tea.

"Oh wow! Intelligent, beautiful, and creative! Poor Pete would have asked you out if he wasn't such a racist." Kane gave a chuckle, the light sound letting her know he'd spoken without malice.

"Men like him are a dime a dozen. I can't say I'll ever get used to it but I've learned how to respond in a manner that keeps everything calm." Damesha felt a bit uncomfortable talking to a stranger about the issue, but Kane was different.

Damesha had dated quite a few men in her life but nothing serious and she'd quickly left them in the past. The way Kane looked at her was somehow different.

"That's just not right, not how you should have to live at all."

"That's life. You either accept it and get on with life, or you explode and cause yourself more problems than it's worth." Damesha cut herself off as the waitress brought out the most delicious Buffalo wings she'd ever smelled.

"These smell gorgeous!" she said as he picked one up.

"I tell you what, meet me back here later and I'll buy you all of them you can eat." He looked at her with a question in his eyes.

"Sure." She didn't even have to think about it. She'd never considered eating chicken, or with your fingers to be sexy but she felt a quiver low in her belly as she watched him eating. Sensual and slow, his movements had her enthralled.

"Great. You staying over at the motel?" Kane pointed across the street at a rundown but clean motel.

"I guess I am. I'm Damesha by the way." She realized they hadn't introduced themselves yet and held out her hand. With a laugh she pulled it back, his hands were covered in orange sauce.

"I'm Kane Alexander. Nice to meet you, Damesha." He gave her a happy smile and went back to eating. Damesha had almost got in her car and drove off after the incident with the policeman, but she was glad she'd stuck around. This Kane Alexander was intriguing.

Damesha and Kane spent the afternoon at the restaurant, sitting under the umbrella as the sun moved across the sky. Though she was normally quite private, Kane coaxed her life story out of her. She told him about the hard-luck choices of parents, how they'd both ended up in prison, as they walked Annie then went back to their table.

"Mom took the fall for the man that fathered me and died of a drug overdose in prison. Dad fell off the face of the earth and it was left to my grandmother, to raise the baby girl my mother had left behind. I was two when my mother died. My grandmother is the only mother I can actually remember." She had told the story so often for scholarship boards and magazines that the words came out almost monotone now, as though she was reading out loud from some other person's story, not her own.

"My parents never married so I have her last name, same as my grandmother's. She used to put me to sleep with stories from the past. We lived in a pretty rough part of Brooklyn, Grams kept me on the straight and narrow and steered my future with those stories." Damesha's eyes had taken on a faraway look as she remembered the large, loving woman her grandmother had been.

"What was she like?" Kane asked, his eyes gleaming with curiosity.

"Oh, she was beautiful, wonderful. In her early days she'd been a jazz singer, and was quite famous for a while, but music is fickle. She bought her apartment and saved the rest. She was still getting royalty checks but they grew smaller over the years. We struggled, but we made it. Instead of hanging out on the streets at night, I studied. I wrote stories and got myself a college scholarship. Then I left Brooklyn. Now, a few years later, here I am. I'm not rich but I'm not doing bad." Damesha looked down at her hands on the table. Writer's hands, long and limber from all the typing she did.

"Not bad at all. Wow. What a tale!" Kane wanted to know more about this beautiful woman. It wasn't just a physical beauty that drew him, he realized, it was something inside her; a strength, and a sense of dignity. He knew those were important to her.

His family would not approve of his liking an outsider. Kane gave off an air of genteel poverty, a man fallen on hard times, but that couldn't be further from the truth. And he knew a thing or two about the woman Damesha was researching.

"I'll tell you what, I know the homestead this woman, Elspeth Fighter as we know her, built when she came here. She came just at the end of the Border Wars, when the people of Kansas were still fighting over the state being a state free of slaves, where people were truly allowed to be free. She came to this area because it was barely settled, hoping for some peace. I can talk to the family that owns the property, see if they'll let you view it." Kane wanted to help her but he also wanted to see her again. He really enjoyed her company and didn't care if his family approved or not.

"So she changed her name! That'll be why we lost track of her. She was known as Effie Beauchamp in Louisiana. Oh, I'd love to see the house!" Damesha had been stunned to learn the woman had changed her name and hadn't immediately answered Kane's question.

The woman, Effie, had disappeared when she came to Kansas. There were reports that she'd made it to the area but not much about what had happened to her once she'd arrived. Damesha had suspected she'd changed her name but couldn't find out what the new name was. That was part of the reason she had come to Kansas, to find out what happened to the woman that led over a dozen slaves out of the swamps and into Kansas. It was a great tale to tell, but she needed to know what happened to her once she arrived in a state still reeling from its own terrifying war over the issue of slavery.

Damesha was amazed that one of the first people she'd spoken to about the woman had filled in the blank. Now she not only knew the woman's name, but was going to visit her house. Descendants of the slaves Effie had led out of Louisiana had given the name of the town but had known little about what happened to her. Most had moved on, uncomfortable in a state not sure about the status of the people that escaped to it for freedom.

"So do you know what happened to her? Did she survive? What kind of life did she have?" Damesha reached into her handbag for her phone to record Kane as she asked him questions.

He saw the voice recorder go on and didn't protest so she left it rolling. Damesha smiled at him gratefully.

"She had a family and advocated for abolition. That made life hard sometimes, the homestead is actually the third one she built. The first two were burned to the ground, but she survived."

Damesha's visible shock told him she would be investigating more about the matter. "Life wasn't easy back then for anybody, but especially those that bucked the trend. Elspeth definitely did that."

"It sounds like you knew her." Damesha's eyes were tender, curious.

"No, but I've heard a lot about her. She was a truly pioneering woman." Kane's voice trailed off as he stared off into the distance.

Damesha realized the sun had gone down and flushed with embarrassment.

"Oh dear, I've taken up all of your day. I hope you didn't have anything important on?"

"Not really. I was just going to go out and check some fences. It'll keep." His brother would be pissed, but the older Alexander brother would just have to get over it.

"I guess I need to head next door and get a room. Thank you for everything today. You've, well, you've really been a huge help in so many ways."

"Glad to be of service. Here's my cell number, give me a buzz when you get ready in the morning and I'll meet you here. And maybe tomorrow night we can get that dinner?" He gave her a teasing smile that made her knees wobble a little as she stood.

"I'd love to! I'm just going to take Annie for a walk and settle into my room for the night. I'll definitely call you in the morning." She gave him a happy grin and shook his hand before he walked to his truck. An old beat up thing, the truck had seen better days. Damesha didn't care if the man was poor or not, she liked him.

With a happy little wiggle, she gathered up her things, paid her bill, and settled Annie into the car to drive across the road. An hour later she was writing in her blog about her day, Annie had been fed and walked and was happily napping at her feet on the bed. All was well with the world.

After days of driving and long nights of sleepless-ness, Damesha settled into the comfortable bed with a dreamy smile. Annie, not content to sleep at Damesha's feet, scurried up from the bottom of the covers and plonked herself beneath Damesha's chin.

Damesha resettled them both and sighed in content-ment. Her hair was still wet from a very hot shower, and all she wore was a towel. The memory of Kane's warm, tingle-inducing voice played in her head and she thought about turning on the recording she'd made earlier just to hear it one more time. That led to a thought about calling

Kane to come over and him catching her still in the towel, but fell asleep before she could even reach for the phone. The final thought led to some naughty dreams though.

* * *

DAMESHA HAD breakfast with Kane the next morning and, same as the night before, did a lot of laughing. They ate outside under the umbrella once more and Annie was a very happy girl because she had her own plate of bacon. Soon, they were driving out to the homestead and Kane was telling Damesha about the place.

"It's kept by her grandchildren and great-grandchildren, but there isn't much property left. Over the years the current owners of the ranch bought up parcels until all that was left was just the house. They signed an agreement with the family that they'd all work to maintain Elspeth's memory and her home. It's an important part of local history and national history."

Damesha was pleased Kane sounded like he really cared about the place. They bounced as the truck wound its way up a long and very bumpy dirt road. The windows were down and the sun bright, a perfect summer day, unlike in New York where you could sit in your apartment in a sweater if you wanted to run the air conditioner to death. Damesha pulled her shoulder-blade length hair back, tying it up.

She watched the scenery going by and patted Annie as the dog pushed across her lap to shove her nose out the window. The dog lapped happily at the rush of air and they all rode in comfortable silence until the homestead came into view.

Weathered boards, maintained but aged to a silver gray, decorated the house in clapboard fashion. Two stories tall, the house was oddly narrow but there were windows on each side of the house.

"She didn't need much but light was one requirement," Kane said as he pulled up to the house. "We put sealer on the wood but Elspeth never painted the house so we don't either."

"You work for the family?" Damesha asked as she got out, already taking pictures.

Kane scratched at his head, pushing his ball cap back for a moment and then gave an affirmative sound. "Something like that, yeah. Let me show you the inside."

Damesha missed the awkward moment, too enthralled with the house. To the modern eye it wasn't much, she'd seen barns that were better constructed but there was something about the house, sitting out here on its own with a large willow tree in the front yard. She wondered if children had swung from its branches.

Annie followed Damesha around and into the house with a questioning sound.

"We're just staying for a little while, baby. Let's have a look around." Damesha calmed the puppy and moved through the house. Four rooms on the bottom, four on top, sparsely decorated but clean and free of dust.

Damesha moved to the living room where several old black and white pictures decorated the wall above the fireplace. "Are any of these Elspeth?"

Children, adults; a variety of people populated the old portraits but Damesha had never seen a picture of Effie, the woman she was now calling Elspeth. It was the name she chose for herself; after all, Effie was her slave name. Kane walked over to the picture and pointed at one of an older woman with a tiny baby draped all in white, or what could only be taken to be white in the colorless picture.

Her face was deeply lined and Damesha thought some of them must be scars they were so deep and ragged. Her eyes shone out defiantly though, and Damesha felt a connection to the woman with her hair wrapped in a scarf in a plain black dress.

Usually, Damesha's visions, psychic ability, premonitions, whatever you wanted to call them, came in the form of flashes of disasters, large and small. From an early age flashes of buildings burning, car crashes, and other accidents had plagued her. She'd even seen the boulder tumbling off the hillside and crashing down on her fifth-grade teacher on a class field trip before it happened. She'd learned to hold her tongue about the things she saw at an early age, people didn't like being told how they were going to die. In this old house now, with her senses straining to catch anything, she caught something like an echo, a memory of a life lived. Pain, heartache, and misery but also strength, joy, and love. Walking back over to Kane Damesha felt the moment slip away and she looked back at the picture.

With a sigh and a last push to concentrate, Damesha held her hand over the picture, straining for a last echo of something, anything, that might tell her more about the woman.

"She looks strong," Damesha said.

"Yes, I suppose she was bound to be after all she'd been through." Kane pushed his cap into his back pocket, a habit it seemed, and walked into another part of the house.

"I, uh, talked with the family that owns the property now. Not many people come out here anymore, just descendants wanting to show their children about Effie. There's a guest house the ranch owners built. They've said you can stay there while you do your research if you want."

Damesha followed Kane into the next room. There was a large wardrobe, an old brass bed covered with a handmade quilt that was obviously quite old. As she looked into Kane's beautiful eyes, Damesha found herself wondering how comfortable the bed was.

"You can stay there tonight if you'd like." He looked down into her blue eyes, lost in their color for a moment, but then she smiled and her bright white smile distracted him.

Damesha took a shuddering breath as she saw his eyes fall to her lips and stepped closer to the man. Just one kiss. His lips came down to hers, drawing closer, and Damesha felt her heart stutter. It was going to happen.

The bedroom door slammed shut as a breeze blew through the house.

"Oh!" Damesha gave a startled cry and jumped away from Kane.

"Right, let's get out of here for now. We can come back tomorrow when we bring your stuff over. Do you want to see the guest house?"

Damesha knew from the missed moment that she needed to stay in the strange smelling motel room with the lumpy bed. At least for one more night, especially after all those dreams she'd had about Kane's strong naked body to the moonlight. She felt her pulse quicken at the thought and she turned to Kane with a guilty smile.

"I've paid for tonight, might as well stay there. Shall we have dinner?" Damesha called for Annie and walked out of the house to the truck. She didn't mind romance but if she didn't watch she was going to be in bed with this man in no time at all. She was here to write a book, not for a romp in the hay.

3

Damesha stared in amazement at the brown folder sitting on the table in the amazing guest house Kane brought her to that morning. Guest house, right, it could be operated as a small, luxurious hotel there were so many rooms. The entire front of the place was covered in clear privacy glass, giving a gorgeous view of the surrounding landscape.

The file was far more interesting though. Damesha opened it, forgetting the sadness she'd felt when Kane turned down her offer of a cup of coffee. He had things to do today he'd said, his hands stuffed down in his pockets as he gave her an apologetic look. Let on her own, she'd wandered around the house.

Now sitting in the kitchen with the file, she read the note on the top. In handwriting she didn't recognize, the note said the files had been passed down through Elspeth's family but they'd left them with the ranch owners in case other family members or researchers showed up looking for clues to the woman's life.

Damesha went through the file, working to catalog each piece, making note of useful information and a week later she had a full outline. Elspeth, the free woman, had had an eventful life, not just through her advocacy work, but in her private life. She'd had three life-partners, stating often that she'd never make herself a slave in any way, including marriage. Elspeth saw marriage as a woman giving herself to her husband, becoming his slave, and she refused to ever be a slave again. That didn't stop her from having eight children or holding her head up high.

Elspeth was a crusader, a woman who understood her own worth, and wasn't afraid to kick out the first man who tried to beat her into submission one night. She went out and found a pitchfork in the shed, running him off her property. Damesha learned all of this from newspaper reports. The first partner had been laughed out of town when he complained to local law enforcement. A woman running a man off with a pitchfork, the sheriff had scoffed, then told the man it sounded like he'd deserved it.

That incident had endeared Elspeth to many, but a

few in the area were still full of hate and a need to cause mayhem. They hadn't liked Elspeth writing tracts about abolition, and some simply hated the fact that she could read and write. When local papers started printing Elspeth's work her house was burned down. Undeterred, Elspeth pitched a tent until a new house could be built. The second house was nicer. By the time it came to build a third one, Elspeth had learned her lesson and built a serviceable home that would not be hard to replace.

Damesha was in love with the fiery spirit and resolve of the woman and gazed down at her outline with pleasure. It was going to be a joy to write. If only Elspeth had kept a diary! Damesha made a note to ask Kane about that later. She hadn't seen Kane all week but she was hoping to see him this weekend.

A tolling of the doorbell brought her back to the present. She went through the house, down a long hall and to the front door. She saw Kane through the glass and smiled as she opened the door to him over burdened with bags.

"Speak of the devil! What's all this?" Damesha laughed as she took a few of the bags and went through to the kitchen. Kane kicked the door closed and followed.

"I come bearing food and groceries and get called the

devil, what's up Damesha? You don't love me anymore?" Kane teased, setting his bags down on the long table, away from Damesha's obvious work area. "You know we have an office for work right? On the second floor?"

"Oh, I was just thinking I hadn't seen you, and then you show up! I know there's an office but I feel more at home in here. Now, what's all of this for?" She looked at the bags, pulling items out.

"The family said you haven't left the house all week and told me to go get you some groceries before you starved to death. Been busy have you?" His grin let her know he hadn't minded shopping for her.

"I'm in absolute heaven! There's so much information in the file! I've been creating an outline for my book because I've decided it's going to be full novel-length. I've lost track of time. In fact, I don't think I've eaten today. Shall I cook something?" She gave him an inviting smile and he sat down gratefully.

"I'd love that! I got two steaks to cook on the grill in hopes you'd invite me for dinner. Shall I get it started?" He headed to the back door which led to a deck with a full cooking area and a pool.

"Sure! I'll put this stuff away and see what I can put together for us." Damesha was happy to take a break from work, especially when one that included Kane's company.

An hour later they had steaks, Spanish rice, refried beans, and a salad set out on a table outside. They each put food on their plates and spent a few minutes enjoying the food.

"You made that rice? I don't think I've ever had Spanish rice that tasty!" Kane looked as though he'd been transported to heaven as he mixed a little of the rice with the beans.

"It's good isn't it? A lady my grandmother knew taught me how to cook it. She was from Mexico so she taught me how to cook the stuff found in restaurants but also the real deal too. Between my Grams and Isabelle, I learned a lot about cooking."

"I'm just going to take a room upstairs and let you cook dinner every night then!" Kane sipped at his beer as he spoke, a teasing light in his eyes.

He put his hand down on the table and Damesha couldn't help brush it with her own. Their eyes met as sparks flew between them. Damesha took a deep breath.

"That might be a good idea. You could use some fattening up." The man was perfectly fit but Damesha couldn't think of anything else to say.

"Arf!" Annie was beneath the table waiting for the morsels of delight to fall her way. She was usually very quiet, never even barking, but if she wanted some attention she'd make a small sound.

Damesha fussed at Annie with a kiss to take away the hurt and gave her a piece of gristle she'd saved. Annie licked her human and chewed happily.

"Tell me about you Kane, I can't let you move in until I know more about you, can I?" Damesha meant it to be teasing but Kane shifted uncomfortably.

"There isn't much to tell. I was born and raised here in Henderson. I have quite a few siblings, brothers and relatives. I work for the ranch, live not far away, and I'm thirty-two years old." He put more food on his plate, not looking her in the eye.

"Did you go to college?" Damesha prodded, hoping to learn something more.

"Yes, I have a bachelor's degree in agriculture." He stuffed his mouth with food.

Damesha wondered if his unwillingness to answer in depth was because he was married. There was no evidence of a wedding band on his finger but in today's world that didn't mean much, not everyone wore rings now.

"Do you have a wife? Children?" She leaned her head towards him, probing for answers he did not seem very willing to give.

Kane almost spit his food out. "What? No! Neither. Oh man, no, not at all, not even a girlfriend."

"So why don't you want to talk about any of your

family? What are you hiding?" She poked him in his ribs, a bit put out he was so reticent in answering.

"Nothing! I just don't get on with all my brothers very well. I'm a bit of a black sheep really." For a moment he looked away and Damesha saw something like hurt darken his features before it slipped away.

"Ah, trouble-making bad boy are you?" Her eyes glittered at him as she tried to keep that darkness at bay.

"Not at all. It's politics, really. We just don't see eye to eye on how things should be done and who should be in charge of matters that impact everyone."

"Oh, I hear you. Politics can be killer in families." Damesha did not have any family left that she knew but her friends had called her more than once in tears over a fight with their own family members.

"That it can. Especially when, well, let's not get into politics ourselves." Kane finished his food and pushed his plate away.

"No, I suppose we shouldn't. What a lovely sky." Damesha looked up at the night sky. "I can see the Milky Way. You never get to see that in the city, there's too much light pollution."

"I guess that wouldn't be a bad thing if you were afraid of the dark. But how do you get to sleep with all the light?" Kane was looking at the stars himself, finding the planets and constellations as his gaze roamed.

"Oh, we use blackout curtains and anything else we can find to block the light out." Damesha turned for a moment holding her hand out to Kane in a "don't you see" sort of way. He mistook her meaning and gently took her hand. At his touch, Damesha felt peace flow throughout the rest of her body. It wasn't a fluke then, Kane really did bring her peace. Sort of. Her heart started to race and she could feel heat rising into her cheeks so he disturbed her in other ways.

Damesha's breath halted in her chest and she looked away, shocked at how much she enjoyed holding his hand. She was far from a virgin, but Kane made her nervous with the thoughts that filled her mind as his strong, warm hand took hers.

Picking her drink up with the other hand she went back to stargazing and let her thoughts wander. This wasn't so bad, out here in the country. Sure, she could not call out for any meal that she might desire, she wasn't near public transport, and everything seemed so far away but it was peaceful, quiet. Taking a deep breath she closed her eyes, her left hand warm in Kane's, comfortable. No this wasn't bad at all. It actually felt like home, the first place that had that feeling since her grandmother passed away.

She went to take another drink from her bottle and realized it was all gone.

"Do you want another drink?" she asked, turning her head to his. She saw him start and open his eyes. He looked over at her with a smile, but shook his head.

"No, I'd best head home for the night. It's getting late. I'd like to take you to a real, genuine, honest to God swimming hole tomorrow though, if you'd like to get out of the heat and into some real country. I like swimming pools but there's something about a natural swimming place that just can't be beat. You game?"

"Well, yeah! I can't come all this way and not experience a swimming hole, now can I? Awesome!" She'd have to dig out a swimsuit from somewhere, she remembered seeing some down in the laundry room, maybe she could borrow one. "I can't wait!"

Kane stepped up to her just before he walked out the door and something told her he was going to kiss her. Maybe the heat of awareness in his eyes, maybe it was the way his lips parted slightly as he stepped up to her. A noise outside stopped him though and he turned away.

"Is that a wolf howling?" Damesha asked, frowning.

"Yeah, we have them here. We sometimes get a lot of…strange animals here." His face had gone kind of funny for a moment but he caught himself. "I'll see you tomorrow, then."

"Yeah, thanks for the groceries and everything. It's

been a lovely night." She gave him a grateful look before he got into the truck and disappeared.

Damesha stood waving as he drove away, her mind wondering what would have happened if they hadn't heard the wolf howling. She knew it wasn't going to help those dreams she'd been having but she was kind of starting to look forward to them. She hadn't had sex in a very long time and those dreams were hot.

She reminded herself once more she wasn't going to be here forever but the memory of Kane's eyes as he looked down at her pushed the nagging voice aside. He might be poor, he might live in a different state than her, but he was oh so tempting. Grabbing one more beer from the fridge, Damesha went back out to the back porch. No, life wasn't bad here at all.

* * *

KANE CURSED as he steered the truck to the ranch house. He knew what that howl had been about. He was being summoned by his big brother. He wanted to punch the steering wheel. No, he wanted to punch his brother, but knew that would not go over well with the family. It would not go over well at all.

Pulling up to the front of the house, a monstrosity of local wood and rock piled together to create a mansion,

Kane stopped the truck and got out. He had a few secrets he was keeping from Damesha, secrets he simply couldn't tell because too many lives depended on keeping them. The fact he was one of the people that owned the ranch wasn't necessarily a secret, it was just something he hadn't mentioned yet.

He walked into the house, scuffing his boots on the rug outside to knock off any dirt, and walked past the winding staircase in the large front room to a door beneath it. Cade's Lair, that was what Kane called it. His brother's lair. Cade was the eldest of his brothers and the leader of the clan. His word was law, but Kane often bucked it.

Kane pushed open the door and entered his brother's office, a dark room with little light filled almost to the brim with furniture and books. The office was where Cade did most of the family business.

"Nice of you to answer the call, little brother. Have a seat." Cade waved at a chair in front of his desk.

"I'll stand. What do you want Cade? I was kind of busy." Kane leaned against the closed door, his arms crossing over his chest. His face was a mask of boredom; a mask he'd learned to adopt a long time ago. Cade could be tough, Kane knew the man had to be, but that didn't mean he had to like it.

"That's actually why we called you in here. You need

to stay away from that woman. Don't distract her, don't go falling in love with her, don't have an affair with her. Leave her alone. Take her food, show her around, then leave her be. She isn't for you. She's not one of us."

Cade had noticed his interest then. As Kane suspected, his family didn't like his new interest either. This was his warning, stay away or face the consequences. He didn't mind consequences, he decided.

"I'll tell you what, you mind your own damned business and I'll mind mine. Laters, Cade."

"You'll do as you're told, Kane. You're my business. This family is my business."

Kane stuck his middle finger up over his head as he walked out the room, heading for his own house. He didn't have time for this.

4

Bright morning sunlight filtered through the curtains, piercing Damesha's eyelids, rousing her as Annie snuffled at her neck, wanting out already. Damesha stretched and scratched at Annie's ears, giving her a kiss on her head before she slid out of bed.

"Let me go myself, sweetie, then I'll let you out. You are such a good girl, baby, yes you are." Damesha padded through the house after she sorted herself and then let the bouncing dog out into the yard. Annie ran around joyfully, loving the chance to sniff out who had come to visit the night before and where they might have wandered.

Damesha watched the dog investigating the grass and trees for a moment, then went to the kitchen to take the French press from the cabinet to make some coffee. She needed to try on that bathing suit and maybe pack a lunch before Kane arrived. She felt a shiver go down her spine as she remembered her dreams about the man.

"At least I'll find out if dream Kane looks anything like real Kane today," she said to the coffee press as she pushed down the plunger. "I hope he looks like dream Kane."

She laughed at herself then went through the house to the laundry room, sipping at her coffee. She spotted the bathing suit she'd had in mind, brand new with a tag still on it and read the sign over the washing machine.

All items left on the premises may be used by other guests. If it's hanging on the shelf marked "abandoned" you may take it. Fair warning, check for all of your belongings before leaving.

Damesha thought the note was clear enough. She checked the size and looked it over. Pulling her nightgown over her head she pulled the strapless tube of a swimsuit up over her body and knew it fit. She headed to the nearest mirror to look.

The brown material cupped her breasts alluringly, while the high cut of the thigh showed off her legs. With golden buckles at the waist, the suit looked expensive, elegant, and Damesha loved it. Declaring it hers, she went back to the bedroom and found some shorts and a loose top to put over it, and slipped on a pair of sandals. Going back to the kitchen, she prepared sandwiches and other snacks and put them in a hamper she found on a shelf.

Damesha was prepared when Kane showed up. Annie was ready too with her travel bowls and her own blanket. They were both waiting on the porch when Kane pulled up. Damesha had to smile when he got out of the truck, light blue swim shorts came down to his knees and a white tank top covered his broad chest. She had never seen him in anything but jeans and a t-shirt. He looked good in shorts.

The shirt revealed bronzed shoulders and arms with well-developed muscles Damesha wanted to squeeze. And his calves! The man had the most beautiful legs, just as bronzed as the rest of him, with a light covering of hair. He chuckled and Damesha looked up, wondering why he was laughing.

"I'll ask again since you seem to be fascinated with something near the ground, are you ready? Annie's already in the truck." His bright white smile distracted her again.

"Hmm? Oh yes, I'm ready!" She felt heat rushing to her cheeks. "I, uh, I made us some lunch as well."

Carrying the basket with her, they went to the truck and Damesha reminded herself she was an intelligent, grown woman, not a horny teenager who'd never seen a hot guy before. She cast a glance to Kane, reversing the truck to head back to the road. Even his toes were beautiful and most men had horrendous feet!

Looking away from Kane, she watched the scenery speeding by. They were heading to an area she'd not been to before. She thought about the time she'd spent with Kane so far. That first meeting and how they'd instantly clicked. Damesha wasn't the type for holiday flings but maybe just this once. She snuck a look at him before turning back to the window once more.

He was a beautiful man, but also funny, intelligent and kind. Maybe just this once she could let herself go, take some pleasure for herself. Then she'd get back to work, she'd throw herself into it and have Kane out of her system. Something told her it wouldn't be that simple, though.

Kane took a right turn to a secluded area of the reservoir where the grass ran out and turned to a small beach with a wide expanse of water. He got out of the truck, leaving the windows down as Annie jumped out after him, running straight for the water.

"Annie!" Damesha called but stopped to laugh as the dog took a flying leap and splashed into the water. She was now happily paddling around, her face happy and relaxed. "I guess she likes water."

"It would seem so. Let's unload this under that grove of trees and then we can do our own diving in. The water is slightly saline so just keep that in mind. There's a water hose over by that little outbuilding, we'll have to rinse the salt water off of her. The salt will give her problems if she tries to get it off herself, but she should be fine to swim in it." Kane carried a cooler, a bag, and an umbrella down to the trees and Damesha followed with her own bag and the basket.

Kane showed her around the area, a clearing more than anything, and they set up a picnic area about ten feet from the water. Kane threw himself to the ground, looking up at her with his hand held out to help her down.

"This patch seems fine for resting on, Damesha. And if you like ants, well, you're one lucky lady because I think we might have put the blanket down on a nest or two." Kane laughed as he brushed the several insects from his legs and they moved the blanket to another spot.

Settled once more, the pair watched Annie running in and out of the water, chasing her own reflection, as they ate under the shade of the trees overhead.

"Why isn't there anybody else out here?" Damesha asked, putting her plate back in the basket after finishing her sandwich and potato salad.

"It's Thursday, most people are at work. There's a new public pool in town with giant slides and waterfalls so all of the kids go out there now. It's mainly young families that can't afford the pool fees and older folks that come out here. Oh, and people like me, traditionalists that would rather swim in a little salt than chlorine." Kane gave her a slow grin that made her knees wobble even though she was sitting down. One of his incisors was just a little bit crooked she saw now, an imperfection that made him even sexier somehow.

Damesha looked away, her heart pounding frantically in her chest. She wanted to lean over and kiss him, but was afraid he'd reject her. She told herself that was stupid, he'd invited her out here, flirted with her mercilessly, and was giving off strong signals that told her he was interested. But something held her back.

She suspected Kane had secrets, deep secrets that he didn't share with anyone. He was still very quiet about the family that owned the place, about his own family, and about his past. She also sensed something in him that made her feel nervous, edgy. There was something raw, animalistic in him that he kept under guard. Damesha had seen it with that cop on her first day, a light in his eyes, an expectation of being obeyed, that had sent a shiver down her spine.

Oddly for her, the quality intrigued her, rather than

repulsing her. Damesha sat back, letting her hair tumble under her head as she came face to face with Kane.

He looked into her eyes, his so dark they looked black, and hers a clear light blue. Both stopped breathing as their longing grew and Damesha's hand came up to brush his smooth tanned cheek, his lips parting at her touch.

"Damesha?" His word came out as a whisper and she put her finger over his lip.

"Not yet." She felt uncertain, still unsure about starting this but knowing that it was somehow inevitable, this time with Kane was meant to be. "You're hot, let's swim."

Kane gave her another one of his devastating grins, his black hair falling into his eyes, and sat up. He tugged the tank top over his head and threw it to the ground as he stood, running straight for the water with a whoop of joy.

Damesha laughed and pulled off her own clothes, walking more sedately into the water. She loved to swim but it wasn't something she often did in the city. Diving under the water once she'd reached a deeper depth, Damesha swam under the soothingly cool liquid, slicing through the water easily.

She finally came up for air and found Kane looking around for her. "There you are!"

Brushing her hair back from her face, she smiled and splashed water at him. "I'm like a fish when I get into water. I love it!"

"That's fine with me. I love that suit by the way. It does lovely things for you." He gave her a dirty grin and stared down at her small but still pleasing chest.

At five foot eight inches Damesha was pretty tall for a woman, so the water wasn't too deep for her closer to shore but out in the middle, she couldn't feel the bottom. Looking down at her chest she realized treading water was also doing "lovely things" for her as Kane had put it. Her skin glistened in the sunlight and her breasts moved up and down as her arms waved in the water.

"Well, you're not so bad yourself in those shorts of yours. What's that tattoo by the way? I hadn't noticed it before." Damesha felt a cold wave roll over her as she swam closer to Kane, but the water was still and no current flowed to explain the cold. The coldness was inside of her. She'd seen that tattoo in her dreams about him. In the middle of his chest a circle decorated with black ivy encircling a stone door with round iron handles. It was an odd choice for anybody but Damesha was too shocked to worry about the oddity of the tattoo.

"I...oh wow...uh..." Damesha's words trailed off as she looked into Kane's eyes and then swam away.

She was out of breath by the time she got back to the blanket and plunked down, staring at Kane as he followed.

"What's wrong? Why did you go all weird on me?" He dropped down to sit beside her and examined her face.

"Your, uh, your tattoo. I've dreamed about it." She could feel the heat in her face and tilted it down towards her knees as she pulled them close to her chest. She hadn't suspected the dreams had been a part of her abilities, just an example of erotic dreams people sometimes had.

"What do you mean, dreamed about it? As a place or as a tattoo?" He didn't seem shocked just curious to know what shape it had taken.

Damesha knew the whole thing was weird and knew she should demand to be taken home and fly straight back to New York, but something kept her in place. Kane, he kept her there, he drew her and she just couldn't resist his draw. How could she explain how she'd dreamed about the tattoo when she'd never even seen it?

"It was on your chest, you were, ahem, naked. I touched it and it kind of, well, lit up." She pushed a finger against his flesh now, the muscles beneath tensing and moving as her finger slid down the six-inch circle between his nipples. He had a very broad chest she noted. A very tempting chest.

Unlike her dream, the tattoo didn't light up as she touched it this time. It stayed the same black and white ink, a plain but complicated drawing of a door. The calmness of Kane's presence soothed her and she closed her eyes. She could smell a faint scent, cologne maybe, and drew nearer to see if it was. She inhaled deeply before looking up into his eyes.

Her lips parted slightly, revealing a trace of pink on the very edge of the inside of her lip. It was a tempting sight, though she didn't know it. Kane moved towards her, his own lips parting, his own breath hitching as her hand flattened against his chest. He twitched when the nail of her pinky finger brushed his nipple accidentally.

The world disappeared as their lips came together, as though a wall of darkness swooped in to make them the only being in existence. Damesha felt the soft give of his lips, the heat escaping from his mouth just before his wet tongue slid along her bottom lip. Damesha's head fell back, but Kane followed, moving over her body, his chest pressing against her breasts, cold in the wet suit.

Their skin quickly heated up as hands began to move, exploring curves and long stretches. Damesha's hands slid down his strong back, learning every muscled inch. Kane's slid down her long waist, memorizing the curves and dips of her torso before splaying over her hip.

Damesha clung to him, a hunger building in her for more. The taste of his kisses had her sucking at his lips, pulling the tender flesh between her teeth as her legs parted, and he moved to settle between them. Her eyes opened and she felt as though there should be light pouring from them. Intense wasn't even the word for it.

Their eyes locked together before Kane gave her a devilish grin full of dirty promise. Oh, this was going to be one fun ride! Moving down her neck, Kane nipped at the spots he found that made her whimper. When he sucked on the place where her neck met her collarbone, her hips wiggled, pressing into him.

Kane's lips moved, his hips sliding as he moved down Damesha's body, seeking out the dark mounds within the confines of the very beautiful bathing suit she wore. Damesha gasped as his smooth chin pushed down the material, brushing her nipple before his mouth closed over the bud. Her hands went straight to his black hair, holding his head in place as the wet heat of his mouth sucked at her, drawing deep on the tight flesh.

Damesha couldn't stop her legs from wrapping around his waist, the narrowed section between his hips and ribs the perfect place to grasp him. She ground against him, pushing her heated center into the ridge hidden by his shorts. But she knew it was there and she wanted more as he continued to draw on her nipple, sending pulses of pleasure straight to her core.

Her eyes flew open as he suddenly disappeared, the warm air somehow cool against her superheated skin as he started gathering their things up. Damesha sat up, confusion creasing her brow, as he threw things into the basket and called for Annie.

"Come on girl, let's get you rinsed off, it's time to take your Momma and introduce her to my house. We're going to need far more privacy for this."

Damesha gave a low laugh of relief and started grabbing at things herself. A bed sounded nice. And if it got the rest of his clothes off then she was all for it.

5

Kane drove quickly back towards the guest house, but pulled into a road Damesha didn't remember seeing before they reached her house. She saw a forest of trees but not a house. Within minutes, a large log cabin came into view, two stories tall, and made from local wood. Nice, but not what she was interested in at the moment. They hadn't even put all their clothes back on, just threw their things in the truck, loaded Annie up, and left.

Kane stopped the truck and stared at the house. Had he changed his mind? She looked at him, worried that she was about to get a rejection speech. With a long expulsion of air, he turned to Damesha.

"Are you sure this is what you want?" He turned to Damesha, his eyes questioning her, probing her face for any sign of uncertainty. "Because we aren't going in there to play poker and watch videos, we're going in there for sex. Possibly a lot of it. No, I guarantee you, there's going to be a lot of sex."

Instead of voicing her answer, Damesha opened her door and got out, letting Annie follow her. She walked up to the door and turned to look at Kane, still sitting in the truck. His eyes narrowed for a moment and then he was following her. Damesha waited patiently as Kane opened the door and Annie ran straight in, settling on a couch she found in a room off to the left.

Kane shut the door and Damesha had time to notice that the house was well-appointed in dark masculine tones before he began stalking her, backing her up to the pine staircase that led to the upper floor. Damesha backed against it with a grin, bringing her arms out to embrace him. His lips found hers as they fell gently to the steps and pushed the remaining scraps of clothing they wore away.

Damesha felt the heat of Kane's silky body between her bare thighs and couldn't stop what was happening if the house had caught on fire. A need unlike anything she'd ever experienced took over, driving her to suck at his tongue as his hips thrust into her crevice, his long hard flesh sliding between her damp folds. She moaned her delight as his movements tantalized her, fuelling the fire burning in her depths.

They didn't speak, couldn't speak because their mouths were too busy tasting each other. Damesha's hands stroked Kane's back as his roamed over her body, to her hip to pull her close to his hard length. Damesha wanted him inside of her, she needed his hot hard length buried in her depths, but Kane had other plans. Moving down her body, Kane found her breasts and teased a dark nipple, his tongue flicking at the peak until Damesha pressed into his face, a light sound of pleading escaping her lips.

Kane gave a low chuckle of satisfaction and encircled the nipple inside his hot mouth. Damesha moaned as the heat surrounding the tender bud sent shocks of pleasure throughout her body. A tension was building inside her core, and her senses were fading away.She wasn't aware of the faint sunlight changing in the room, or that a bird was singing just outside of the window. All she knew was Kane. His smell, his touch, and the need to feel more of him.

Her hands roamed, reaching for the long length of his cock but he brushed it away with a muffled sound of protest. He wanted to focus on her. She leaned back on her elbows, letting him have his way. If he wanted to pleasure her she wasn't going to stop him.

Kane's fingers teased at her other nipple, and Damesha writhed beneath him, his cock so close but still too far away.

"Kane." His name was a plea, a demand, whatever he wanted it to be, she just needed him. But Kane wasn't done playing. He obviously wasn't in the mood for quick sex.

"I've waited far too long to taste you, Damesha. Don't make me rush," he whispered to her before he slid down the steps, kneeling at the right height to throw her left calf over his shoulder and bury his face between her legs. His lips closed over her, sucking up her feminine taste.

"OH!" It wasn't expected but was certainly welcomed. She cried out again as his tongue replaced his lips. The hot tip plunged into her folds, splitting her open for his desire.

Damesha's hands went to his head, holding him in place as his mouth found the spot that made her cry out his name. She moved her hips with his movements, her hips writhing as she quickly approached the heights of pleasure.

With a humming vibration, Kane voiced his own pleasure at her reaction before sliding his two middle fingers into her hidden pink flesh. A sudden tensing of her ass and Damesha was exploding around his fingers, her body quivering from the pleasure of his fingers and tongue in her folds.

Kane clung to her, his arms wrapped around her thighs to keep his head in place as she rode his face, her cries of pleasure making him thicker and harder. Damesha could only hang on to the step beneath her as it felt like her body tried to turn inside out. The waves washed over her time and time again, but eventually started to dissipate. Kane slowed his movements, waiting. As she rode the last wave he plunged into her deep and hard.

A muffled groan of pleasure escaped from his throat and Damesha opened her startling eyes to pin his gaze with hers. They stared at each other as Kane thrust into her over and over, his pace quickening as her gasps grew louder.

"Oh, that's it baby, give it to me. Give me more, Kane. Give me all of it." She urged him on, her hips thrusting to meet his. Damesha had never been shy about sex but Kane just brought something out in her, a need to voice her thoughts, to make demands and ask for what she wanted. He made her bold.

Damesha sat up, her body agile and lithe, cupping his ass as he slid into her, demanding more from him. Damesha held her face up to his and his lips captured hers, his tongue plunging as deep into her mouth as his erection plunged into her receptive body. She felt an unexpected wave pass through her as her walls clenched around his length and let her head fall back as Kane's stroking made her inner walls pulse once more.

Kane gritted his teeth, breaking the kiss as she came around him, and finally gave up the fight to hold back his own orgasm. He let all the sensations flood over him, into him, as he felt her wet heat, smelled her scent on his face, tasted her tang in his mouth. Then he looked down into her eyes, and let go.

Damesha held him, reveling in the sensations of Kane's pleasure. She could still feel him pulsing inside her, feel his body shuddering, the goose bumps along his skin. She could hear the gasps and groans of pleasure, and felt her body tingle in response. She held him close, smelling his scent, tasting his sweat as she kissed his neck, the salty liquid clinging to her lips.

He worked to catch his breath, loving the moment, enjoying it more. Another new experience. Usually, after sex, she was in a rush to get to the shower, wasn't the kind that needed cuddling and talking. Kane was different though. He made her feel different, and she responded to him differently. He made her feel love and that shook her.

As he sat up and looked down into her eyes she knew she might be in trouble. There was something in his eyes, something she'd never seen from another person before. Somehow she knew her own eyes reflected that same emotion. She thought it was love and that was definitely going to cause trouble. Pulling him back down to her lips she pushed the thought away, telling herself to stop being silly.

Kane followed her lead, letting her up when she pushed against him, leading her to the bedroom. She found a bathroom—bigger than her entire apartment— behind a door, and found a walk-in shower that gave her ideas. Turning a wicked smile in Kane's direction she started the shower, adjusting the water to a heat she liked.

He gave her his own grin and followed in after her, pulling her close as the water flowed over their heads. Damesha let his lips linger on hers, enjoying the way Kane kissed her, sweet but erotic. He knew how to draw his tongue along hers in a way that was suggestive but not obscenely funny. His lips sucked with passion, not a need to devour. Gentle, she realized. Kane was gentle.

Sitting on the dark blue tiles of the shower seat, Damesha crooked a finger. She wanted to taste him and make him weak. Grasping him tightly but gently, she moved over him, taking him in slowly. Her tongue slid along his length as he braced his hands against the wall, pressing himself deeper into her throat.

"Damesha. Oh baby, that is so good." Kane's groans were met with moans of delight from Damesha and it almost became too much to withstand. He pulled away, and Damesha took the hand he offered. They rinsed off and she followed him into the bedroom.

The biggest bed she'd ever seen was in the middle of the room, curtained off with white linen. He pushed a panel aside and helped her climb up. He followed and Damesha giggled as his damp skin met hers.

Rolling together in the bed, Damesha stopped laughing as Kane's lips covered hers, heat building in her lower abdomen with each stroke of his warm tongue. Opening her legs wider she felt him sliding against her slick heat and moaned up into his mouth.

Kane groaned in response and pulled her close to his hips, snuggling them together as he ground down into her. They both gasped and Kane flipped her with a flick of his wrist, his strength on display for a moment. Damesha grinned as Kane positioned her. Oh yes, this was going to be all kinds of fun if he was always this adventurous.

His tongue slid up the roundness of her bottom before his fingers sought out her moist entrance. His fingers slid into her for a moment, a sound of approval letting her know he was happy with what he'd found there. Damesha bucked into him, her body starting to become tired and sore, but gluttonous for what Kane had to offer.

She felt him shifting behind her, and then he was inside her, his long length plunging into her depths. For a moment his hips were melded to her bottom, their bodies fitting perfectly together. They started to move together, no more holding back, no more trying to prolong the pleasure. It was a greedy moment they both worked hard for, striving for that explosive release.

Kane's fingers gripped her hips tightly, and Damesha grasped a pillow as Kane pounded into her from the back. Then the world turned into pulsing pleasure as her body tipped over the edge of into oblivion. She gasped his name one final time before she was lost.

6

Three weeks later, Damesha stretched in Kane's bed, her body relaxed, languid. She had known the word 'relaxed' before, but had no idea what it really felt like. Sliding her legs under the silky cotton sheets, her feet found Annie. Damesha sat up with a smile, throwing the covers off, and stepped down from the bed.

Annie followed with a gentle snuffle, her tail wagging as she went to find the flap in the door Kane had installed just for her. Damesha went into the shower, knowing she was in love and happy. It was more than just the endless nights of passion; the days spent trying to concentrate on her work that let her know she was in love. Kane was a smart man, he asked her questions about her writing, making her brain work to dig deeper for answers, to see beyond just the news-paper print or the diary pages.

He also made her laugh, his sarcasm and dry humor a refreshing bite rather than tedious. They often had discussions that people might take for arguments but they were happy debating. They challenged each other and though they didn't agree on everything, they respected a difference in opinion.

Kane was making her grow, making her mind expand, and she loved that about him. She loved how he supported her and allowed her to support him. She even loved the dark side of him, the side that still wouldn't tell her everything, that part of him that went broody sometimes in the night. She'd find him at the window staring into the darkness outside his bedroom. She'd entice him back to bed and chase his shadows away.

Things were getting tense with his family. She didn't have much interaction with them but she'd heard the phone calls Kane tried to hide.

"When is she leaving? When she feels like it. What's it any of your business? She's not at the cabin now, she's at my house. Well, she can go back to the motel if that's how you feel about." Kane paused, listening to the reply. "That's real nice, Cade. Nice. Thanks a lot, brother."

Kane had then used some words Damesha had rarely

heard him use and had to smother a giggle behind her hand. That told them.

She avoided the stares of the family when they drove into the yard, never coming into the house. She'd go inside to avoid them when she was at his house. She assumed, of course, that the problem was her skin color. Without more of an explanation from Kane it was all she could assume. He'd only say that they were old fashioned, that they didn't like outsiders. She didn't particularly care what they thought, but sometimes Kane would turn aloof and she wondered if it was all getting to be too much for him.

Annie came in, heading straight for the kitchen. Damesha followed, calling after the dog.

"And what would madam prefer for breakfast this morning? Pancakes, French toast, gravy and biscuits?" Damesha patted Annie's head as she knelt in front of her. Annie gave a low woof as Damesha said gravy and biscuits so Damesha assumed that was what she wanted.

Damesha had dressed in a loose pair of pants with a thin cotton top and was preparing Annie's requested breakfast when the sound of a car pulling into the driveway startled them both. Damesha went to the front of the house to see a man she recognized as Kane's eldest brother stepping onto the wide front deck. The house wasn't too different from the cabin she'd been in but the deck went all the way around the house and had more privacy with the use of less glass.

Damesha stood at the door, staring at the man through the glass. Something told her this wasn't going to be pleasant. With a grim set to her mouth, she opened the door as the man stared back, giving her the creeps.

"Hello, Kane isn't home. Can I help you?" Her tone was superior, her left eyebrow crooked. She looked the perfect picture of domestic civility but the coldness in her eyes gave away her true thoughts. Smoothing a strand of hair behind her ear with well-manicured nails, Damesha hoped she gave off the impression that she didn't care what the man wanted.

"Hello, Damesha, we've not been introduced. I'm Cade, Kane's brother. I just thought I'd see if you were getting ready to go home yet? I can help you pack and get your papers in order if you need." A not so subtle hint at all from the man. His grin was just as fake as hers, she noted, her eyes taking in every slight twitch around his mouth and eyes. No, he didn't like her any more than she liked him. He'd caused the mutual dislike, though, not her.

Damesha stepped back and looked at him. Remarkably similar to Kane, Cade was a little bit taller but less handsome. It wasn't really a matter of looks, it was how his face was set. Something cold and hard lived inside

Cade, something Kane didn't have. Oh, Kane was arrogant enough, independent and headstrong, but he lacked the hard edge Cade had. And rather than making her feel calm, this man sent her senses into overdrive and anxiety made her chest tighten. Pushing it all down and controlling herself, Damesha looked at the man with a raised eyebrow.

"I'm not planning on leaving just yet. I'm sure Kane can let you know of my departure, though. If I leave." She started to shut the door but Cade stopped her by putting his hand out.

"*If* you leave?" Something in his tone told Damesha she shouldn't have pushed so far. Oh well, she'd done it.

"If I leave, yes." She didn't give a toss what he thought and refused to back down just because he wanted to be a little aggressive with her. He didn't pay her bills. He could take a flying leap. "If you'll excuse me, my breakfast is burning. Have a nice day."

She didn't stop to see the stunned expression on Cade's face. She shut the door and locked it. Turning away, she went back to the kitchen. Her hands shook as she took the biscuits out of the oven and removed the sausage from the pan. Okay, so now adrenaline wanted to hit her, she could live with that. She'd just put Cade in his place. Maybe he'd leave Kane alone now. Something told her that wasn't going to happen but she could hope, couldn't she?

Placing the breakfast on a plate, she put Annie's biscuit and sausage in a bowl to cool and sat down with a glass of orange juice. She wasn't certain she wanted to get in some kind of Romeo/Juliet scenario with Kane's family but she knew that he was worth fighting for. A hard worker that was generous, loving, kind, and everything she'd ever wanted Kane was totally worth fighting for. Thinking some of her own dirty words at the memory of Cade, Damesha finished her breakfast and went back to work. It wasn't worth worrying about.

Working throughout the morning, Damesha started putting together the research she'd done into a folder so she'd know where she was using each piece in the book she was planning. She made copies of quotes, highlighted passages, and indexed all of it. While she was busy with her book, Kane was out riding the fences on a four-wheeler, making sure the cattle were healthy and not breaking down the fences. Kane wasn't a hired hand, as Damesha had thought, she'd learned that much anyway.

No, he was one of the owners of the ranch, along with his siblings. Damesha still didn't know a lot about them, other than there were three other brothers. She knew their names and that Cade was the oldest of the four boys. Men. Oh, they were definitely men, Damesha reminded herself, though she had yet to see the other two brothers. If they were similar to Cade and Kane then there was no doubting they were grown men.

Cade was a beautiful man, sexy in his own right even, but he didn't appeal to Damesha. There was too much dominance in his gaze for her liking. An independent woman, she had no need for a caretaker or a surrogate father. Kane was an Alpha male, but he wasn't a dominant male. He was a capable partner and that was more important to Damesha than anything else. She didn't need a man like her father who'd run out and leave her mother in trouble in more ways than one.

Damesha decided long ago sex was a good thing but relationships with men, leaving yourself vulnerable that way, wasn't for her. Now she'd made herself a liar. She knew she was falling fast for Kane, but couldn't stop it. Maybe he was the one, the fabled one who'd bring her to her knees. Tapping a finger against her lip, she paused what she was doing. Damesha looked out the kitchen window at the Kansas wilds. Could she live here?

Looking at the forest outside she knew she could. She loved it here. She really cared about Kane and he'd insisted she stay with him rather than staying at the guest house. He was willing to go that far but was he willing to keep her for good? They hadn't really talked about the future other than Damesha's work. Did he want her to stay? Did she want to stay?

"What do you think, Annie? Do you prefer life here or in New York?" Damesha looked down at the dog at her feet.

Annie's answer was a look that screamed "Are you stupid?"

"I guess that answers that then. You prefer living here. I bet that's because of all the bunnies and stuff you get to chase around."

Damesha considered the question as she prepared dinner later, a role she'd taken on happily when she'd seen the state of the art kitchen in Kane's house. She spent most nights at his house now so she'd started cooking for him. She loved to cook and the kitchen was like something out a dream. Putting the lasagna she'd prepared into the oven, she stared out of the windows once more.

When Kane came in through the back door of the kitchen, Damesha had the dining room table set and the plates filled with salad, garlic bread, and lasagna. Two glasses held a dark ruby red wine that would stain their lips but tasted divine. Candles lit the room with a soft intimate glow. Damesha had a question to ask Kane, the mood needed to be right.

Kane ran upstairs to shower and change clothes,

quickly coming back down to sit with Damesha. She'd dressed carefully in a white sundress that highlighted the darkness of her skin while somehow making her eyes stand out. Not one for makeup, Damesha only needed her natural beauty and a good hairstyle to take Kane's breath away. He walked into the room with a delighted smile.

"What's the occasion?" Sitting across from her, rather than at the head of the table, he picked up his fork to taste the food. "Excellent. I can't believe how good of a cook you are. You have it all, why do you need me?"

His tone was teasing and Damesha laughed as she sipped at her wine.

"Well, there's one or two things you provide that I can't do myself." Her tone was just as teasing but it had a naughty hint to it that got his attention.

"Oh? Just a couple of things huh?" Kane kept eating, waiting for her to expand on those things she needed.

"A few maybe. But now it's time to make a decision. I've finished my research and I'm ready to start writing the book." She stopped speaking and looked at him in a pointed way. "I can go home now. There's nothing to keep me here."

Kane's fork dropped and he looked into her eyes. Damesha wasn't sure if they showed hurt or sadness but they weren't filled with relief either. That had to be a good sign. She was nervous, unsure how any of this was going to go, and her heart was pounding because she was afraid Kane would reject her. She'd made up her mind this afternoon, she wanted to stay here and give it a try. She could work from anywhere in the world, she knew in her heart she wanted to see if they could make a life together.

"I don't understand." Kane put his fork down to take a sip of wine. Wiping his mouth, he looked at her with hurt tempered by a tiny bit of anger. "Are you saying you're going home now, there's nothing here for you?"

"I don't want to presume, Kane. I know men don't like to get too attached, that they prefer to keep their freedom." The words sounded too similar to the words she'd said about her father and she could see by the way his jaw tensed that Kane was remembering the last time she'd spoken those words. "I just don't want to put you in an awkward position. Your brother came by today to remind me it was time to go home."

"Cade was here? I see." Kane sat back in his high-backed dark walnut chair and stared across the table at her. "This is our goodbye dinner then."

"That's up to you." Damesha let the words come though she knew they made her sound weak and needy. It was up to him. He had to make a choice.

"Right then." Kane stood, his dinner forgotten for the

moment as he began to walk out of the room. He stopped at the arched entrance and looked back at her. "I guess I'm going to have to spend the night making you squirm then. Show you why moving in with me is a good idea."

He walked out the room then and Damesha quickly followed, unsure if it was an invitation to come and stay permanently or for just another holiday romp. She ran after him, following him up the stairs, calling out his name.

"Kane, stop!" She'd followed him to the stairs but stopped as he walked up. "What does that mean?"

He stopped at the top and waited for her with a grim look on his face as she started to follow him. Damesha paused at the third to last step and looked up at him uncertainly.

"What does that mean exactly?" Damesha looked down as Annie ran past them, determined to get in her own bed if the humans were going to bed now.

"There's nothing holding you here? That's what you said right?" He stalked down a step, his gaze stern and unreadable.

"Well, yes, but I meant there's no work here for me to do now. I have all of the pictures I need. The files have all been copied and compiled. I can't find anything more about her in the county's files. My work here, at least, is done." She bit her lip, needing to say more but afraid of swaying him in a direction he really didn't want to go in. This had to be his choice, his choice made freely and without her influence. That was the only way to ensure he wouldn't change his mind later and leave her. If he wanted her enough to ask her to come back then he meant it.

"Oh, so it wasn't just a 'thank you for the sex, I'm out now' kind of speech you were giving me?" He pulled her up the final step, stepping back until they bumped into the wall.

"Not at all, Mr. Alexander, not at all." Damesha threaded her long slim arms around his neck and held her face up to his. "It was a question."

"Ah, a question. It didn't sound like one." He pulled his head back to give her that slow sexy grin of his as he waited for a reply.

Damesha felt her knees wobble, something that happened often around Kane but had never happened before in her life. She threaded her fingers through his hair and gazed at his lips. Moving in close, almost touching him, she began to speak. Her lips brushed his as she said the words but she didn't press into him further.

"Where is this going, Kane? Do I go home and try to

forget you or do I stay and we make a go of this?" Her left eyebrow crooked, her eyes meeting his.

Kane shuddered in her arms, his breath a hungry whisper across her lips. His tongue flicked out, moistening his dry lips, brushing hers as it did so. Neither moved, neither spoke.

Kane breathed deep, his chest pushing against hers before he crushed her to him, his hand going to her head to press her lips into his. Their kiss was desperate, hungry, but also joyful as they both gave their answer in the form of a kiss. Kane's tongue sought out her lips, asking for entry. Damesha opened, allowing him in as her own tongue tangled with his. Each stroke sent shivers down her spine, but he broke away. Damesha wanted to protest but Kane cut her off by picking her up and carrying her to the bedroom.

"I suggest you go back to New York then. You'll need to pack your things before you come back here." His words came out as a growl against her stomach as he pressed her down to the bed, lifting the hem of her dress.

"I'm not coming all the way out here to Kansas without some kind of promise, Kane. I don't need marriage but I need to know we're going to do our best to make this work," she responded, legs spreading reactively to allow him to nestle between them.

"Oh, you go get your stuff, baby. I'm about to make you a promise for life." Kane thrust his hips into her, the hard edge of his cock pressing into her through the thin cotton of his lounge pants.

"That's all I needed to know." Damesha pulled his face down to hers, gasping as he slid into her, his clothes somehow gone but she didn't care how. She was lost in the sensation of Kane inside of her, stroking every inch of her depths. Yes, this is exactly where she wanted to be.

7

*D*amesha sat in her empty apartment and thought about the memories she'd made there. This had been her first real apartment. The first place she'd ever rented on her own, the first place she'd finally felt like an adult, and now she was leaving it. A pang of nostalgia filled her eyes with tears but she smiled and brushed them away. She was heading out for a life she could have never imagined, a life in the last place she'd ever thought of settling. With Kane, even if his family didn't like it.

"Damesha, can I have these yoga pants?" Erika wandered out of Damesha's bedroom with a pair of gray pants. "I might be able to get into them."

"Sure, whatever you want. I don't think I'll be going to any yoga classes way out there anyway." Damesha looked at her friend with sadness, knowing she wouldn't see much of her now. "When are you coming out?"

"As soon as I can afford to. I still can't believe all of this. It's a good thing your lease was up for renewal anyway." Erika turned to the window, looking out at the view of other high-rise buildings.

"It's one of the reasons it was easy to decide to go out there. That and Kane. I can't wait for you to meet him, Erika. He's so wonderful." Damesha couldn't believe she was gushing, actually gushing, about a man. "I know that's what all women say but you'll see when you meet him. He's just incredible."

"Oh, we all say that, yes, but what makes him so special for you, Damesha? Why is this man so great he's taking my best friend away?" Erika turned back to her friend with tears in her eyes. "I want to beg you to stay but I know it's pointless. I've never seen you smile like that."

"Come here, honey. Sit with me. I don't know why I'm so tired today." Damesha put her arm around her friend and they cuddled together on the couch, snuggled against each other as only friends can do. "I'll be back to see you. I have to bring this country boy to the city sometime. And you'll be visiting."

"I know, but what is it, Damesha? Why is he so

special?" Erika sniffled from under Damesha's arm, wiping at her nose with a tissue she found in her pocket.

"He's handsome but it's not that. I think there's too much to list really. If I had to narrow it down to one thing? He's a stand-up kind of guy."

"Stand-up? What, he's a comedian?" Erika looked at Damesha with confusion.

"No, he's the kind that stands up for you. If someone's acting like a jerk, he takes care of it. A protector. Is that better? He's always making sure I'm alright, he keeps an eye out for me and protects me. I've never had anyone do that before." Damesha lost herself in memories of Kane once more and realized she missed him terribly.

"You really love him, don't you?" Erika broke into Damesha's thoughts.

"I think I do. This whole thing is different. It's unlike anything I've experienced before. That has to mean something, doesn't it?" Damesha looked to Erika for an answer.

"I suppose it does. I know I've never seen you like this. From the pictures you've sent me I can see that you and Annie are both happy. I can't believe he installed a doggy door just for Annie!" Erika had to grin at the thought. "She isn't even his."

"Oh, don't tell her that! She's claimed Kane just as

much as she has me. She adores him! They're always playing with each other, walking outside, it's beautiful really."

She missed Annie too, her constant companion. It just wasn't the same without Annie at her feet when she went to sleep and woke up. Or between her and Kane. They'd made it a joke between them, her and Kane, that Annie was their birth control dog, enforcing the no-puppy making zone as frequently as she could. Poor Kane had even been on the receiving end of some very reproachful looks from Annie after she was kicked out of bed. The first time they'd seen Annie give him those looks had been hilarious and she'd spent the entire day giving him the evil eye when he'd go near Damesha. They'd wondered if Annie thought Kane had hurt Damesha she'd seemed so upset with him.

Damesha's heart melted as she thought about Annie back home with Kane. She was probably wondering where Damesha was. This was the longest she had been away from Annie since she'd adopted the dog. She knew she missed Annie dearly and she'd only been gone a few days. She missed Kane too but for different reasons.

"Oh, there's that look again." Erika stood up, picking up a box and her handbag. "Let's get this down to the shipping truck and get you out of here. Then you can get back to the guy that puts that look on your face. You have a flight to catch don't you?"

"I have one more stop to make then I'm going to the airport. Thank you for helping me, Erika, and not giving me a fit." She hugged her friend before picking up the final box in the room. "It means a lot to me that you've been here for me."

"Always, my friend. And if this doesn't work out you know you can have my couch any day of the week." Erika smiled as they walked to the lift.

"I'll remember that." Damesha chuckled, dreading the moment the elevator stopped at the bottom. That was the point she'd part ways with Erika for a while. It had already been four months since she'd seen her friend. They'd spent the last three days together packing up her apartment but that wasn't long enough. "You sure you won't just follow me out?"

"I can't right now, honey. I have a protest to organize this week, and then get it off the ground. But soon, I swear." Erika hugged her friend before the doors opened, but then let her go. "Besides, you're going to need some alone time with that hotness in Kansas, aren't you?"

"I guess so. But I don't want to leave you!" The women handed the boxes to the man in charge of the shipment truck and then embraced.

"It won't be for long, I promise. I'll be out before you know it. Now go. I don't want to cry in the street. We're New Yorkers, aren't we? We're supposed to be rude, not sappy." Erika pushed her away with a watery grin. "Go on. There's your taxi. Get going, girl!"

Damesha ran over to the taxi but stopped before she got in. Waving at her best friend, she remembered over a decade of memories in a second. With one final kiss blown from her palm, she stepped into the car. She hoped Kane appreciated what she was giving up for him because it was an entire life she'd just walked away from for him.

With tear-filled eyes she watched Erika until the car moved too far away and turned a corner, hoping her appointment at the doctor went quickly. She'd made the appointment before she left Kansas. A fatigue was plaguing her and she had no idea why. Damesha was worried she'd picked something up in that reservoir, a brain-eating ameba or something. It didn't matter how much she slept, she was always tired lately.

Or maybe something was missing from her diet now. Iron or something vital like that, maybe she needed supplements. She'd find out soon enough. Within a half hour, she was sitting in the doctor's office, the cab agreeing to come back when she finished. She followed a nurse into the exam room, giving the woman the information asked for.

"Date of your last period?" the woman said absently as she typed Damesha's previous answers into a small laptop.

"Just a few weeks ago, I think. Um, let me check." Damesha's head started to swim as she realized she couldn't remember having a period the month before. She pulled out her smartphone, checking the app she'd installed to keep track of the dates. She could never remember exact dates so she'd started keeping a record of it a few years ago.

The nurse waited patiently as Damesha started her phone, opening the app up to see a screen with a warning in large letters.

"119 Days Late!"

Damesha's fingers went numb as the phone dropped from her fingers to the floor.

"Ah, I think we have an answer perhaps?" The nurse picked up the phone and turned to Damesha with a sympathetic look on her face. "Are you alright?"

"I...uh. Whoa. I think I need a pregnancy test." Damesha felt like an utter idiot for not realizing.

"How late are you?" the nurse asked, going back to the computer with calm and efficiency.

"Apparently 119 days. How could I not have realized?" Damesha went back over the last few months in her mind. She and Kane had grown closer as she spent her days writing and the nights making love. He'd come and drag her out of the office they'd set up when he thought her day had been too long, even when she protested about being in the "flow".

They'd take Annie out for long walks, spent free time swimming, kissing. Then she'd go back to writing and the world would disappear as she lost herself in the world she was creating in her book. Time had slipped away and one month had turned into another. She'd woken up one morning and realized her lease was almost up on her apartment.

It had been time to go back to New York but she hadn't wanted to leave Kane. She'd started to worry about her exhaustion but put it off to long nights and longer days of writing. Change of environment and diet could be causing it, she'd told herself. Anything but the one thing that had been so obvious.

How was she going to tell Kane? Damesha went through the motions for the rest of the hour she spent at the doctor's office, giving the samples requested without complaint. When the doctor came in to confirm her pregnancy, handing over papers she'd need to take to a doctor in Kansas, her mind finally woke up.

"I'm pregnant?" she asked the doctor standing in front of her.

"Yes, Damesha, you are. Congratulations." The man smiled down at her, obviously used to stunned young women sitting in her position. "It'll take a while to sink in, but you'll be fine. Just make sure you get some prenatal care in Kansas."

He patted her hand as Damesha walked out with an expression the doctor also knew well. A secretive smile women had when they knew they were pregnant but nobody else knew. A look of wonder and awe that made people turn around because it was such an intriguing look.

Damesha had arranged for her flight in the evening because she hadn't known how long she'd be at the doctor's that day. She had hours to kill and decided that maybe now, when it was too late, to finally do some research on Kane. She knew he had money, that his family had money, but surely just a ranch wasn't enough to make that much money for four grown men? The money part wasn't a problem, Damesha had her own after all, but not like Kane. The problem was she barely knew anything about him.

He'd always sidestepped her questions and after a while, she stopped asking. The family had stopped creeping past his house, and she'd not overheard any more conversations about her. His past stopped becoming important. But now she was going to have a baby and she needed to know about the man that was going to be her child's father.

Sitting in the airport, Damesha wondered if she'd let love blind her. She was going to have a child and she barely knew anything about the baby's father. She didn't even know Kane's birthday for crying out loud. She started searching for him on social network sites but found nothing. She'd just found a site that offered police reports and old addresses that looked like it might be useful when an older woman sat down beside her. The woman made no bones about staring at Damesha's screen.

"Going off to meet your internet boyfriend, are you? I tell you in my day we didn't do such nonsense. And if you're only just researching him now, well, you've put it off too long." The older woman, about eighty dressed in a yellow track suit with a headband in a matching yellow looked like she was about to go jogging not go on a flight.

Damesha looked at the woman with annoyance. "Excuse me?"

"You young folk nowadays. You run off all over the globe looking for love but you never think about the long run. What's the person bringing into your life?

What do they have to offer? Are they worth your time? Will they be there for the hard times? Young people now, you let your hearts rule too much. Sometimes you got to think with your noggin." The older woman pointed at her head and winked at Damesha.

Damesha knew the woman was trying to be helpful and let her annoyance wash away. "Oh, I've actually spent the last four months with this man. But as you said, I was thinking with my heart, not my head."

"I see. Well, at least he's real for you. Some people wander off and find out the person never existed after spending a fortune on a trip they couldn't afford to begin with." The woman made a sound with her tongue in her teeth while shaking her head. "That's never a good idea."

"Oh, it's nothing like that. I'm just going back home." Damesha didn't feel bad about the slight fib; after all, Kansas was home now. "I don't know a lot about him though; he keeps his cards close to his chest."

"Some men are like that, I've learned over the years. That's not always a bad thing. Sometimes the quiet ones are the thinkers, the problem solvers. He might just be a keeper, you know." The other woman's eyes, old and rheumy, still sparkled and Damesha felt a reassurance she hadn't felt since her grandmother passed.

"You think so? Just a minute ago it sounded like you

were trying to convince me not to go." Damesha wondered what had changed the woman's mind.

"Never mind me, I'm an old woman. It's been my experience, though, that the quiet ones are usually the best ones. He'll talk, when he's ready." The woman got up and looked around absently. "I think I'm at the wrong gate. Have a good trip, dear, and give it a chance. You might have found the one."

Damesha looked down at her laptop for a moment, hiding her tears, and when she looked up to tell the woman goodbye, she couldn't spot her. She turned in her chair, looking all around the terminal but the woman in the bright yellow costume wasn't to be found. Shrugging it away, Damesha went back to the laptop. Shutting the web pages down, she decided the woman was right. Kane would tell her in his own time.

She knew enough about him to know he was a good man. He took care of her as no other person except her grandmother had ever done. He gave her his undivided attention far more than she did for him, and he supported her in whatever she chose to do. Then there was the peace she felt when she was with him. It had disappeared the second she walked away from Kane. It had been painful, letting all those sensations inundate her after so long of keeping them at bay. But what if he didn't want the baby?

Could she have an abortion? Damesha's hand went to her stomach, not even bulging yet, and knew she couldn't do anything to harm it. She wasn't going to judge anyone, but she knew that she simply couldn't do it. No, if Kane decided fatherhood wasn't for him, he'd just have to suck it up. They had a baby coming.

As she sat in the terminal, waiting for her flight to be called, Damesha started to wonder about other things. Why did they only visit two restaurants in town? There were quite a few. Maybe he only liked those two? And where did he go on those jogs he went for at night? Where was he running? Why did he run in the middle of the night? Who did that, even out in a safe place like rural Kansas? It was all so very strange.

Kane definitely had secrets and she wasn't sure she could live with him without knowing them. What if he was a spy or a secret agent? No, that was too far-fetched. Kane just had a lot in his head and he liked to run at night. Maybe his parents had been abusive? As far as Damesha knew both of his parents were dead but she wasn't entirely sure.

Groaning in frustration, she couldn't believe the kind of mess she'd gotten herself into. What was she going to do? It was almost as though she'd been under some kind of spell. Back in Kansas, she'd been curious, but the curiosity had faded, became irrelevant as her feelings for Kane grew. Now, in New York and on her way back to Kansas with far more in tow than just her belongings, reality set in. How had all of this happened so quickly?

"Flight 863 to Wichita is now boarding first class passengers…" Damesha tuned the woman's voice out as she froze in place.

She'd been waiting for hours for this flight, now was the time to make the decision. She could get on and see what the future held, or she could go back to her apartment, renew her lease if it hadn't been taken already, or go back to Erika's. Erika would love to have her back. She could go back to normal, call out for Thai food at two in the morning, get her life back in New York and raise her baby with Annie there as her companion and defender. Or she could be brave.

Damesha was the last person sitting in the terminal when the desk clerk looked up at her inquiringly. Everyone else had boarded. Damesha looked away from the woman, back towards the airport exit. Which way should she go? Standing up, fear tightening her features, Damesha made a choice and took the first step into her future.

8

---

*D*amesha walked through the terminal, so brightly lit the darkness outside was almost day. She hoped she'd made the right decision as she went to collect her bag, trying to remember where the luggage collection was. She followed the signs, nerves jangling and on edge as she drew closer to the area. She reminded herself of the reasons she'd made the choice she had and knew by the time she stepped through the arched walkway that she could have only made that choice, it was the only one that made sense.

Collecting her bags, she quickly walked towards the exit. It was time to go home. Pulling the wheeled luggage behind her, Damesha made a striking figure as she stalked through the terminal; beautiful, but the fierce look of concentration on her face was captivating.

Where was Kane? He had to be here. He'd said he was coming to meet her. Spotting the love of her life in a corner, staring out of a plate of glass and on the phone, she walked over to him quickly with a happy laugh, wrapping her arms around his waist. The moment her fingers touched the material of his shirt she knew the man wasn't Kane.

Stepping back, preparing to apologize, Damesha wondered how she'd gotten it so wrong. When the man turned around her mistake kind of made sense. It was Cade.

"Where's Kane?" Damesha felt a cold sliver of fear pierce her spine, her world beginning to quake at the edges. Yet her normally buzzing senses were quiet. All she felt was the anxiety of not knowing where Kane was.

Cade didn't answer; instead he turned back to the glass, continuing his phone conversation out of Damesha's hearing. She analyzed those few seconds when Cade had looked at her before he'd turned away. Cold burning rage filled those eyes, not sadness or grief. Just rage. What was going on here?

Cade ignored her question about Kane so Damesha wondered if she'd missed the man she was looking for somewhere along the way. The way Cade blanked her made her think he wasn't there for her at all. Maybe he was there to pick someone else up. Slightly embarrassed at the mix-up, Damesha started to walk off, but Cade turned and snapped his fingers at her as he shook his head.

Stunned, Damesha stood there with her mouth hanging open. When he pointed at his feet and made a wiggling motion with his fingers she decided she'd had enough. Turning and walking off, Damesha left the terminal, ignoring Cade calling out behind her.

"Look, there are things happening that you don't know about. Just stop will you?" Cade's voice, so similar to Kane's but oh so different, didn't stop her walking towards a taxi rank, but his arm at her elbow did.

Turning back to the man with an angry slash of her other hand to push him away, Damesha looked into the man's eyes.

"What is so desperate that you can't even get off of the phone to talk to me? And that snapping fingers thing?" Damesha shook her head and turned to walk away. "Oh hell no!"

"Damesha, stop! Kane was in an accident. I was on the phone with his doctors at the emergency room. His truck rolled over on the highway when he came to get you. He's not in good shape." Cade's cold façade broke for a second, his voice thick with emotion, but then he caught himself. His back went straight again and the cold mask returned.

"What? Accident?" Damesha's vision narrowed to a thin tunnel where all she could see was Cade standing in front of her, then narrowed even more until all she saw was his eyes.

"Come with me, we'll go to the hospital." Cade's fingers were far more gentle this time as he took her elbow once more, and helped her with her bags before taking her to a waiting car.

Cade opened a door as a driver popped out of the front to take her bags. Damesha slid into the luxury town car, not noticing how supple the leather of the seats was; only trying to take in the meaning of Cade's words. Kane had been in an accident, things didn't look good.

Damesha felt cold inside, deep down inside of her abdomen and she knew she should be sobbing, crying, begging for answers but somehow she'd gone still instead. Her brain could only analyze those few words Cade had spoken, nothing more. She almost felt as though she was a robot that had been turned off. All emotion had fled, all that remained was cold reality. Kane was hurt.

The sights of the city passed her by, unseen and forgotten as she sat numbly staring ahead, only vaguely hearing the words Cade spoke on his phone. He'd taken it out before the car had even pulled away, speaking in a low forceful tone. He wanted someone to do something; he didn't care what it cost.

Damesha sat silently as the miles rolled past. Soon enough they were entering a hospital's parking lot, pulling up to the emergency entrance. The driver popped around to open the doors. Cade didn't say a word as he strode through the sliding doors and into the brightly lit reception area. They took an elevator up to the fifth floor and Damesha followed along quietly, still too numb to speak. How had she not known? She'd had visions her whole life, not always of fatal accidents, why hadn't she known with Kane?

Cade stopped at a closed door and pushed the handle. Damesha followed him into the doorway but didn't enter the room. Another virtual clone of Kane stood at his bedside, his face an exact replica of Kane's. The only difference was the lighter shade of his dark eyes, almost brown, not quite so black. Beside him stood a tall blonde man with green eyes. She noticed their eyes only because both men were full of a fury she didn't understand. She couldn't understand why that rage was directed at her either.

Damesha was almost afraid to step into the room, their fury almost a presence it was so strong. They looked like angry dogs, wild and feral, and she wouldn't be surprised if they started snarling at her. Damesha knew they could sense her fear but her spine hardened as she took a step towards Kane's still form. Each step brought her peace, a quiet that blocked out the rage of the now quietly departing men.

They left her with Kane and Damesha took his hand, the only uncovered bit of flesh he had. His head was swathed in bandages that ran even under the blankets over his chest. She pulled the blanket away from his body gently, and saw blood starting to seep through the bandages along his abdomen. Bruising could be seen through the lines of the gauze covering his arms and legs. A sob welled up in her throat as she examined him.

"Kane? Baby, I'm here. Wake up for me, my love." Damesha stared into his face, his eyes, nose and mouth the only parts of his face left uncovered. She hoped he'd open his eyes, needed to see the laughter that always filled them, needed that reassurance. Nothing happened. He didn't even stir.

A soft noise behind her made Damesha turn. A man in a white medical coat was standing at the door.

"He's in a coma. I can't tell you much, you aren't family, but you obviously have a relationship. He has a head wound we had to stitch, ribs broken on both sides, and a very deep laceration to his abdomen. The coma is worrisome, I'll admit, but it's common with injuries like his. I'll let the family tell you the rest if they choose to, but any more than that I shouldn't really tell you." The man, in his late 50s and very short with dark hair and eyes, gave her a kind smile then left the room.

Damesha sat down on the chair at the side of Kane's bed and took his hand once more. Tears flowed down her cheeks and the urge to sob was becoming uncontrollable. She held his warm, strong hand to her cheek and the first squeaky sound of pain finally passed her lips. Her shoulders shook as she bent over his hand, the pain of her heartache pushing her into a bend.

"Kane! Kane, please wake up, baby. I can't lose you, not now. I love you, you know, and we're going to have a baby. You have to wake up. Please wake up." Damesha sat with him throughout the night but he remained motionless.

She cried until her nose blocked and her eyelids began to swell. She could not stop the river of tears, not until she ran out of tears to cry. The nurses came in and changed his bandages, gave him shots into his IV line, and took his vital signs. One brought her some fruit, a carton of milk and a blanket. Damesha smiled vaguely and thanked the nurse, but her eyes never really left Kane.

The brothers came back, sitting in chairs against the

wall, but none of them spoke to Damesha. She could feel a wall of anger behind her but ignored it. As the night passed the anger started to thaw, and melted down to something closer to a simmering resentment. Damesha didn't care, all she could concentrate on was Kane. He was all that mattered.

Kane didn't make any noises throughout the night, he didn't shift in his bed, he just lay there, arms to his sides. Motionless. Damesha couldn't let go of his hand, only allowing the nurses to take it as the night progressed. The darkness outside his private room window started to lighten as the hours wore on, and as the first beam of sunlight spread over Kane's legs, climbing his body slowly, he began to stir.

Damesha made a happy sound and climbed from her chair, pushing the gate on the side of his bed down so she could sit beside of him as his eyes opened and he stared up at the ceiling. His eyes, wobbly for a moment, finally focused and who looked down to see who was holding his hand.

"Mesha," he said, the bandages all but holding his mouth shut. "What's going on?"

"Oh, Kane!" She leaned down to touch the side of his face, the bandages preventing skin contact. "You were in an accident, baby, but you're going to be alright."

"Oh. Okay. Love you." He let his head fall back to his pillow and closed his eyes.

Damesha stood stunned for a moment. Kane had never said those words to her. Was it just the drugs talking? Then she realized she needed to let the nurses know and rang the buzzer. The woman soon came in, checking his vitals once more and checking his eyes with a penlight. She pressed the intercom and when the other nurse at the desk answered told her to call the doctor to tell him their patient was awake. The other nurse's smile came through in the sound of her voice as she said she would.

"I'm glad he's come out of it. I'll call the doctor now." The voice that came from the wall was kind of eerie but Damesha was happy. Kane had woken up!

"He'll be able to go home once the doctor has approved the move. You might want to start arranging transport and he'll likely need a nurse for a few days, just until he's completely out of the woods." The kind woman stood in front of Damesha, stoically ignoring the brothers still stonily sitting in their chairs.

"I'm sure we can arrange whatever he needs. This is just natural sleep that he's in now, right?" Damesha was concerned he could slip back into the coma and the snores now coming from the bed were reassuring.

"Indeed it is, but we'll keep an eye on him until the

doctor gets back." She gave Damesha's arm a reassuring squeeze then left the room.

"I'm awake, I'm awake. Not sleeping, just resting my eyes." Kane protested as Damesha sat back down beside of him on the bed and took his hand.

She looked at the wall of brothers in front of her, not sure of what to say to them. They were all still stony-faced but the anger was gone. They all came to stand on the other side of Kane's bed. She realized they hadn't even introduced themselves yet. Damesha ignored the slight and clung to Kane's hand, watching his eyes as his brothers spoke.

"I'll see about getting you home. One of the drivers will bring you. Hopefully, they'll let you out soon enough." Cade patted his brother's shoulder gently then stepped out of line, heading out of the room.

"Get better little brother. I'm glad to see you awake." The other Kane-clone said before beating his own retreat.

The blond one stepped up and touched Kane's face. "That's the last time you get to do that. Use the driver's we have, they're there for a reason!"

Kane garbled something at him and closed his eyes. When he opened them the other brother was gone and Damesha was all he wanted to see.

"I was coming to get you."

"I know. I guess that's why they're so angry." She sighed deeply before continuing. "We'll worry about that later. Rest, get better so we can take you home."

"I'll be out of here in no time. And yes, I do love you." Kane gave a weak smile before his eyes closed once more and he fell into a natural sleep, not the coma of the last hours. His chest rose and fell, a slight snoring sound coming from his nose. He'd said it again. With meaning this time, not just the grogginess of drugs and just waking up. He loved her!

In a few hours, the doctor arrived, and the nurses began removing bandages. Kane was already on the road to recovery, the deep gash that had been circled on his skin already well away from the edges of the ink marks. Traveling from his lower hip up to almost his belly button, the red line sutured with stainless steel staples marred the right side of his body. It looked painful and Damesha couldn't help but wince as the nurses cleaned it.

His head wound was cleaned and the stitches checked. Damesha wanted to cry as she noticed countless bruises, scratches, and shallow lacerations marring his front and back. Even his legs were covered in deep bruises that would take weeks to heal. He never complained as his bandages were removed and replaced.

Kane just stared into Damesha's eyes, happy to see her once more.

"Do you remember the accident?" Damesha asked after the nurses dropped off their breakfast trays and left.

"Just parts of it. I can remember someone running into me, something running into me, I can remember the impact, I remember sounds more than anything. And you. All I could think of was you until the world went dark and I stopped thinking." Kane sighed before he picked up his fork.

"How did Cade know to come and get me?" Damesha had been wondering it all night but the brothers hadn't said a word to her.

"I'd been to see him before I left. I guess when he was called he knew someone had to go get you." Kane wouldn't meet her gaze and Damesha wondered what had happened in that conversation, but didn't push.

"That makes sense. I guess I've met them now anyway. Sort of." She shrugged, picking at the cold eggs on her tray.

"What do you mean? They were all here this morning." Kane looked confused as he picked up something that could be a biscuit, or a paperweight.

"They were here, but Cade was the only one that spoke to me. They didn't even introduce themselves."

"Oh, that's about to change, as soon as I can stand on my own. I'm not having this anymore." Kane shifted around in his bed, his agitation rising.

"It's okay Kane, later baby. Not now." Damesha calmed him as the doctor came back in.

"Well, for such an injured man yesterday, Mr. Alexander, you've healed well." The doctor looked confused but pleased. "With the nurse your brother's arranging for you, we feel it's safe to send you home today, but you're going to have to listen to the nurse and do everything she tells you to."

Kane looked flustered but agreed. Papers were brought, signed, copies made, other papers given to Kane, and phone calls made. A van arrived soon enough and Kane was loaded into something that looked more like a mini-caravan than a van. Settled into a bed with a strap over his legs, Damesha at his side, they left the hospital that evening and headed home. Finally.

9

Damesha stretched out in the bed with Annie that evening, Annie's warm body a reassuring pressure against her legs. Kane was beside them, the room blessedly cool after the heat of the day, and all was well. Annie snuffled softly beneath the covers, Kane's breath came in gentle waves. She was where she was supposed to be.

Kane had three nurses scheduled throughout the day, the night nurse now downstairs watching television. Kane had tried to insist the woman go home, but Cade threatened to have the doctor drag him back to the hospital when he called to complain. Kane shut up and told the woman how to turn the television on to keep her downstairs.

Damesha helped him into some night clothes,

brought him a glass of apple juice, and they'd settled in the bed to watch television. Kane had tried to start conversations twice but Damesha stopped him. Covered in bruises and with bandages still covering a good portion of his body, now wasn't the time. He needed to heal. He'd murmured he loved her and before long he'd fallen asleep.

Damesha still couldn't quite take in all of the last twenty-four hours. She knew each moment, but she just couldn't believe it. She'd found out she was pregnant only the day before, not just a few minutes ago. She'd thought at the time that nothing more could shake her world. Then she'd had to decide whether to go back to Kane or stay in New York. Then the mad dash to the hospital. How was she even awake?

Settling into the covers and turning the volume down on the television, Damesha prepared to spend her first night in her now permanent home. The weight of it settled on her for a moment and her hand went to her stomach. A slight bulge on the flat plane could be felt there but nothing anyone else would notice. She hadn't even told Erika yet!

Annie snuffled at her feet and made an exasperated noise but Damesha brushed her foot along the dog's back and she calmed. Smiling that secret smile of expectant mothers once more, Damesha reached out for

Kane. His shoulder was cool and smooth in her hand, the air conditioner keeping the room as cold as he liked it. This was going to be an excellent place to raise a child. Kane was going to make an excellent father. This was going to be excellent. She just had to remember it in the coming days because if they were anything like the last twenty-four hours it could be a rough ride.

"YOU'RE HEALING REALLY...WELL, KANE." Damesha was examining Kane's head a week later, wondering if the cut had only looked worse than it was that first night. It was almost freaky how well it was healing. Scary, even. Humans didn't heal as fast as Kane was healing. Not any she'd ever known anyway. It should have taken months for these wounds to reach the level of healing they were at!

"I'm a quick healer. It's my metabolism. That's why I got rid of the nurses after the first day. I didn't need them." Kane stood awkwardly as she moved away from him in the bathroom to put the antibiotic ointment back in the medicine cabinet. Putting his shirt on hid the healing line of lacerated flesh on his abdomen from her view. "I'll be able to get those stitches out tomorrow I bet."

Damesha smiled at him and followed him back to the bedroom, Annie hot on her heels. "What are you going to do today then?"

He'd been sleeping a lot during the day, but yesterday he'd gone out for hours. She assumed he was out walking. He'd come home and slept for hours then gone back out again, this time to Cade's he'd told her. She didn't like him being gone so long, but he was healing so perhaps she shouldn't worry.

"I'll ride the fence-line for a little while today. Annie's figured out the logistics of riding on the back of the four-wheeler with me so I'm guessing she's going with me. Are you going to do more writing?" He wandered up close to her, inhaling her scent as he buried his nose in her hairline at her neck. She'd write for hours while he was gone, preparing chapters, footnotes, and other aspects of the book she was preparing.

"Oh baby, don't do that or neither of us will work today." Damesha laughed and gently pushed him away as his lips grazed her ear but his hands remained at her hips, pulling her to sit in his lap on the bed with him.

"Maybe you should take a break." His lips found her neck, his hot tongue licking at the sensitive flesh.

"No, your hip is still healing. Behave!" Damesha continued to laugh, hugging him close for a moment before standing. "I'm a little jealous of you, you know. You've stolen my dog from me!"

Annie had refused to let Kane out of her sight since they'd brought him back from the hospital and she accompanied him on his wanderings now. Damesha would feel jealous but she knew how hard it was for rescue dogs to trust humans again. If she loved Kane that much it was a good thing. Besides, Annie devoted herself to Damesha when she came home, spending hours cuddled up to her as close as she could get.

"Besides, I have to figure out why I heard a monkey last night so I can't go out with you and Annie." Damesha dropped that into the conversation casually but kept her eyes turned to Kane to gauge his reaction as she sat back in his lap once more.

Kane pulled away suddenly, looking at Damesha. "Monkey?"

"Yes, you hadn't come back from Cade's yet, I was sitting on the porch and I could have sworn I heard a monkey. That doesn't compare to the hyena though."

"Hyena?" Kane's eyes were all but bulging out of his head, his words coming out in a gasp. Damesha looked at him with concern.

"Yes, why? Weird isn't it? It's alright, baby, I'm sure I'm just hearing things, or warping the sound of a passing car into a water buffalo. But the elephant was hard to mistake." Damesha got up from her perch in his lap and went to her laptop. "There aren't any of those animals here so maybe it's something in the house? Maybe Annie snatched some kid's toy. I'll have a look around today in the yard. That's where I'm hearing it."

Kane blinked and got up, distracting himself with putting on his boots. "Yeah, or maybe it's a television or something."

"It's hard to tell but if I catch somebody out there making jungle noises I'm going to be upset."

"I'm sure it's nothing malicious, honey. I'll see you later on. Take care of yourself today, you hear me? Don't stay locked up in your office for eight hours with no breaks! It really isn't good for you!" Kane gave her a stern look before he kissed her, taking away the bite of the look. "Love you."

"I love you too, Kane. Be careful. And don't be out too long, that hip is still healing, and even on a four-wheeler you're stressing it." Damesha's voice came out happy but with a note of steel. He needed to rest.

The words came easily now, simply. They hadn't said the words before the accident, only exchanged some meaningful glances, but after the accident, everything changed. Kane had changed as well. He was still the laugh-machine that supported her but he'd become a little more serious, a little more concerned about what was going on with Damesha. They hadn't necessarily talked about the future yet but she knew from the look in his eyes, the one that shouted that she was his, that they definitely had a future together.

Damesha wandered into her office, thinking over the last few days. Those animal noises were weird, and she only heard them when Kane was out or asleep. That made her suspect whoever it was messing with her was waiting until she was by herself. She'd stopped sitting on the back porch but she could still hear the sounds through the windows when she had them open.

Damesha lost herself in typing for the next two hours, her world zeroing in to nothing more than her monitor and the thoughts in her brain. Her fingers flew over the keyboard, her eyes staring only at the monitor as she typed. Every now and then her fingers would tangle together the way the keys of an old typewriter used to, and she'd laugh, telling herself to slow down. Elspeth's story was just flowing from her mind and she knew it wasn't going to take long to get the first draft done.

Damesha started to feel an ache in her back and shifted in the leather chair she'd settled in, and sat cross-legged. She dropped her feet right back to the floor when she heard a howl pierce the air. Her head swiveled to the window but she didn't see anything. It sounded like the howls were coming from a stand of trees just outside of the house. Was that the call of a howler monkey?

Damesha liked nature programs and had learned a lot about animals over the years, despite living in a city, and she knew that was some kind of monkey outside making that racket. She really wanted to go investigate but her hand went to her stomach instead. She had more than herself to think about now.

Since Kane's crash, she'd wanted to talk about the baby, but hadn't told Kane yet. He was still healing, still getting used to her being there. She'd tell him soon. For now, she was going to stay put and ignore whatever it was out there squalling like it was being beat to death. He could handle it.

A banging noise let her know Kane had come back in but she kept typing for another twenty minutes, wanting to finish out her thoughts on that section. Hitting save on the file, Damesha got up and started towards the stairs. She was considering what they should have for dinner when she got to their room.

"Kane? You in the shower, baby? What do you want for dinner?" There was no answer and the door was shut so Damesha turned the handle. She could hear that the shower wasn't running so she stopped. "Kane?"

Still no answer. She pushed the door open and saw

the room was empty. Where was he? She went through the upstairs rooms then went downstairs. Damesha could find nothing. Kane wasn't in the house. She'd heard the door shut though, and his footsteps. Maybe he went back out?

Damesha checked both of the decks, even the swing in the backyard, but couldn't find him. Irritation prickled at her neck but she pushed it down. He wasn't playing a game, Kane could be fun but he wasn't malicious. As Damesha started up the steps of the back deck she heard the wolf howling once more, only this time it was even closer.

"Oh, that's it! It's time to go back inside!" Damesha looked over her shoulder and then ran back in the house. Something had moved in the shadows of the trees and it looked like the shape of a wolf!

Slamming the door shut and locking it, Damesha pulled the blinds so that nothing could see in through the double glass doors. Running upstairs, she wasn't sure if she was afraid of what could be outside or angry for letting fear make her run like that. Telling herself she was being silly she went back into the bedroom, pulling off the clothes she was wearing. The cotton top and shorts suddenly felt too tight, constricting, so she found a loose dress to put on instead.

Throwing her bra and panties on the bed before

moving to pull the dress over her head, Damesha heard a tiny sound, something odd and out of place. Looking back over to the bed, Damesha felt dread rising in her throat. Something was moving under the thin duvet and skimming along under her panties. If the thought of running had entered her brain she wouldn't have been able to move because her legs were frozen, fear gluing her feet to the floor. Her eyes went wide as the lump moved closer to the edge of her panties, an odd noise like snuffling coming from that area.

Damesha opened her mouth wide, a scream just starting to bubble out her throat and for a moment she wondered if anything would come out. Maybe it would be like those dreams where you're screaming your head off but no sound comes out. And just as the scream forced itself past her closed throat, a tiny white head popped out of the leg opening of the discarded under-wear. The scream died as confusion took the place of fear.

"What the hell?" She stared down at the tiny creature before going to pick it up. The silky fur on its tiny body was white with a few black spots on its head and back. A tail wagging fiercely at its bottom end turned Damesha's fear to a fit of giggles.

"Oh, Annie is either going to love you or eat you in one bite! Where did you come from then? Kane? Kane, where are you, baby? Thought Annie needed a friend, huh?" Damesha paused as she went down the stairs to look for Kane once more. If Kane was home where was Annie?

Kane would never leave Annie out there on her own. Maybe he'd dropped her off somewhere, with Cade maybe, while he went and got the puppy? But if that was the case where was Kane now?

Her frustration levels started to rise again and the critter nestled in her arm started to squirm. Damesha held it up to her face, the tiny creature barely filling her palm. A tiny tongue slipped out and swiped her nose experimentally, tentatively. It sat back and looked at her with acceptance.

"Awwwww!" Damesha's heart melted instantly as the tiny Chihuahua settled in her hand, deciding it was nap time. "Where did you come from?"

Damesha knew Kane wasn't in the house now, it was ridiculous to think he was. Surely he would have sprung out of a closet by now, or wherever he might have hidden, to yell surprise or whatever he might have yelled. No, this puppy had magically appeared out of thin air. She decided that was just as stupid an idea and carried on down the stairs. Right, she was losing it, hearing wild animals and finding unexplainable but adorable pets in her bed. But this puppy felt real, it felt as real as that wolf in the backyard had looked.

Going into the kitchen Damesha couldn't decide whether to laugh or cry. She was sitting thousands of miles from everything she knew, pregnant, and with a man she'd almost lost needing her help. She'd worked hard over the last few days caring for Kane those first days when he slept constantly, working on her book in between checking on him and bringing him food. She was overworked, that was all, it had been a rough few weeks, and now her mind was paying the price.

The puppy still slept, cradled in her hand, and it felt far too real. Nope, she wasn't crazy, this animal was real. But how would she know if she was crazy and imagining all of these things? Damesha had heard pregnancy hormones could make you do strange things, eat strange things, she wondered if they made you see and hear, even *feel* strange things? Shaking off the thought that she was losing her mind, Damesha decided the puppy was real, she wasn't crazy, and somebody was messing with her. Which meant someone had been in the house, at some point.

She quickly found a box to put the tiny dog in with a blanket, and went through the house locking windows and doors. She even locked bedroom doors from the outside with the skeleton keys used in the old fashioned locks. It might have been crazier than thinking she was seeing things, but she felt safer locked away. She wished Kane would come home.

Knowing she'd worked herself into a state, Damesha prepared a cup of herbal tea and sat down to watch the puppy. Whoever it was couldn't be too malicious if they'd brought her a puppy. Psycho killers and stalkers didn't leave cute little puppies, did they? They left dead rabbits and creepy notes, stuff like that, she told herself.

The hours passed, Damesha made dinner, the puppy at her side in his box. She'd checked to see, and the puppy was male. He did a lot of sleeping and was generally quiet as she prepared the meal. He was quiet as she sat waiting for Kane to come home with Annie, he was quiet when the food went cold and Damesha put it all away in the fridge. He only woke up when she carried his box into the living room to wait for Kane. Where was Kane?

Damesha fell asleep on the couch, her face streaked with tears. She didn't have any numbers to call Kane's family and wasn't sure whether she should call the police or not. She'd fallen asleep waiting for him, her fears growing as the hours passed. She was exhausted though, her body and mind too worn out to stay awake. Curled up on the couch her eyes had closed and refused to open. The tiny puppy was in his box beside her, sleeping as soundly as she was.

Around three in the morning, her eyes popped open and she sat up on the couch, her mind finally kicking into gear and forcing her to wake up with one realization. Whoever had left the puppy might have done something to Kane and Annie. If Kane had been hurt, surely Annie would have come home, she was always sniffing around, she could have sniffed her way home. If Kane was staying out, he'd have called her and let her know. No, whoever had left this puppy must have Kane and Annie. And they'd left the puppy to replace them.

amesha was about to call the police when the puppy started to whine and bark at her, his little face in a panic. He pawed at her frantically when she picked him up and squirmed a lot, sniffing at her madly. Realizing the poor thing hadn't been outside all day and that she was probably being very silly thinking someone had taken Kane and Annie, Damesha took him out to do his business. The puppy dashed around the yard sniffing every rock and blade of grass until it finally found one that smelled suitable. He squatted to do his thing but then looked up at Damesha. He looked offended that she was watching and barked at her.

"Oh hush and do your business. You aren't my boss.

You couldn't even fight your way out of a wet paper bag." She crossed her arms over her chest and glared down at him.

The puppy barked some more, giving a growl for good measure. Damesha looked at it and laughed.

"Oh go on now, do what you need to do. A mosquito could bite harder than you." The puppy ducked its head in shame and Damesha felt horrible. "Oh alright then, I'll give you some privacy you little bully."

She turned around and the puppy went quiet. Damesha gave it a few moments and turned back around. The puppy was standing at her feet, his little tail wagging ninety miles a minute. She picked it up and went back into the house.

"Look, if you're going to be trouble you can just go back where you came from. Kane is going to get his ass kicked when he finally comes home, and you're about to get a good talking to. Men!" With little sleep and feeling exhausted, Damesha was close to tears as she went back to the couch and sat down. "Where is he?"

The puppy whined and snuffled around on Damesha's chest, trying to settle. Her breasts were starting to become bigger and the puppy had a good place to rest as he put his head down and whined at her. His large dark eyes were sad and Damesha wondered if he was hungry again. Putting a hand under him, she went back to the kitchen.

She fed him some slices of ham and gave him some water. This being in a relationship thing was proving difficult, she mused as she looked down at the now the sleeping dog. Kane had never done anything like this before so she'd give him the benefit of the doubt, but this was really hurting her feelings. The prick of tears in her eyes made her a little mad; she wasn't supposed to be crying over a man! She left the dog in his box and went into her office. She'd get some work done while she waited. It wasn't like she was going to get back to sleep anytime soon.

Damesha worked for an hour but couldn't get much done. She'd type a few sentences then her thoughts would wander back to Kane and Annie. She'd snap back to awareness and start typing again. She finally gave up and saved the file, deciding to go back to the movie she'd fallen asleep to. Kane obviously wasn't coming back tonight.

Damesha went to pick up the puppy in his box but found the box gone. She looked all over the kitchen but simply couldn't find the puppy, the box, even the bowl his water had been in was gone. A cold sensation of doubt washed over Damesha as she looked around the kitchen. Maybe she was crazy? Or maybe someone was in the house?

She ran straight up the stairs and into the bedroom, slamming the door and locking it. Leaning back against the door, Damesha tried to catch her breath. Her hand over her heart clenched into a fist as she screamed, terror suddenly filling her. Someone was in the room with her!

She turned back to the door, frantically trying to unlock the door with numb fingers as a light switched on. She slumped against the door, knowing something terrible was coming. She was about to turn around and plead for her life when the person spoke.

"Damesha? What are you doing? Stop screaming baby, what's wrong?" Kane was out of the bed and in front of her, his pajama bottoms riding low on his hips. Sexy as ever, safe, fine. And there was Annie, yawning as she pawed her way out of the covers.

"What? When did you get here? Where have you been?" Damesha wanted to scream, tears fell from her eyes, but she wasn't sure if it was relief or anger that made her cry. "What the hell is going on here?"

"Baby, we've been here all night, what are you talking about?" Kane sounded upset, concerned even.

"No you haven't, you went out this afternoon and you have been gone for hours! You and Annie both!" She moved away from him as he tried to take her into his arms, refusing to be placated.

"But Damesha, we came back not long after that. We've been here ever since. You've been in your office all day. You wouldn't even come out for supper and I made pizza for you!" Kane looked hurt as he walked back to the bed, sliding beneath the covers.

"No! That's not true! I looked through the entire house. You weren't here! Just that bullying little Chihuahua that growled at me! I looked everywhere!" She slumped into the bed, knowing something was wrong, knowing how the day had gone. Kane was lying, he had to be. But why would he lie to her? He'd never lied to her once since she'd met him!

Sliding down beneath the covers, Damesha felt Annie move close to her, felt a warm wet tongue scrape her palm, and blinked as the light went out. Had she imagined the entire night? Surely not?

Kane turned the light back off and pulled her close, Annie still managing to wiggle back between them. They'd often joked that Annie was their birth control dog because she was always wanting to be between them. Always.

"Baby, there's no Chihuahua. You're working too hard. Tomorrow you're going to rest, that's all there is to it. No more work for you, not for twenty-four hours!"

Damesha didn't respond, couldn't think of a response, so she just tucked her arm around Annie and Kane, and closed her eyes. Tomorrow she was going to call the doctor. Maybe the pregnancy was causing some issue? Maybe it was whatever psychic ability she had? She'd never really thought much about the ability, she'd accepted it long ago, and accepted that she couldn't talk about it. With that knowledge, she'd decided that maybe not thinking about it too often would be a good idea too. Push it away, maybe it would go away, she'd told herself back then.

Now she had to wonder. Had she done some damage to her own brain by doing that? Sure, others would call her crazy for thinking she knew things, for seeing things, but that wasn't true. She'd proved it by keeping a diary when she was younger. She'd even shown it to her grandmother, but the woman had burned the book in a metal trashcan instead of giving it back to her. No, maybe it was time to see a doctor about what was going on with her mentally.

Damesha fell asleep quickly, but her dreams were filled with nightmares. A tiny Chihuahua whose growling mouth grew bigger as she tried to back away from it turned into a shadowed man, stalking her through the house. That led into a dream of drowning and struggle, trying to escape the water that only grew deeper no matter how hard she kicked for the surface. She woke up the next morning drenched in sweat and fighting with the covers.

She sat up but closed her eyes as she realized it was all just nightmares, nothing more. Maybe even that whole episode with the Chihuahua and Kane going missing had been part of the dream? Damesha got up, nausea making her run for the bathroom as she stood. She hadn't been sick often since she'd become pregnant but this morning she was quite ill. Cleaning her face and her mouth, she crawled back to the bed.

"Good morning, sunshine! How did you sleep?" Kane came in carrying a tray with hot tea, orange juice, bacon, fried eggs, two biscuits and a banana. Damesha ran back to the toilet. "Damesha?"

Kane followed her in and soothed her as she was sick, placing a cold washcloth on the back of her neck and holding her hair out of the way. Damesha would have been grateful but couldn't think enough to form the words. When the spasms stopped and she hung her head on her arms Kane picked her up and carried her into the bedroom. The eggs and bacon had disappeared. He brought her the milky tea and she sipped at it gratefully.

"Thank you, my throat is so raw." She leaned back against the pillows, hoping that was the end of it all.

"Seems we've traded places today. You stay in bed, Damesha. When you feel like it, try to eat something. I'm going to eat mine downstairs so it doesn't bother you. I'll be back up in a few minutes." Kane kissed her forehead and went out the door.

Just like that, the events of the night before were dismissed. It must have all been a dream, she told herself. It must have been part of this being pregnant sickness she was experiencing now. A really long nightmare that just didn't seem to end caused by her illness and pregnancy. That was all.

Damesha didn't stop to think why a normally independent, curious and capable woman stopped questioning what she knew to be real. She just wanted the world to stop spinning and her stomach to calm down. It wasn't a matter of being right or wrong, crazy or sane; right now she just needed to feel better so she could get back to normal.

Damesha slept throughout the day, Kane checking on her and bringing her light snacks. Kane took her short responses, snappy tone, and peevishness as part of her pregnancy. He knew about it but wasn't sure she did. He was waiting to tell her, until the time was right.

Of course, she should have realized by now but things had been hectic for them since they met. The accident didn't help matters. He felt guilty about that but there wasn't anything he could do.

A truck had come out of nowhere, aiming right for him. The large black truck slammed right into him, and he'd tried to swerve to avoid the other truck but it was no use. He'd hit something that flipped him, and had barely escaped alive. Now he was determined to protect himself and Damesha at all costs. Even if that meant protecting her from herself.

He and Annie spent the day downstairs making a cradle for the baby, the baby he wasn't supposed to know about. A man knew these things though, if he was an attentive lover and partner. The signs were there.

A warm feeling had filled his chest since he'd first sensed something was different and it only grew. Kane knew it was love, it had started with Damesha. The baby made it grow more and more. Kane had never known these emotions, these feelings, but he knew what they were. His own family was cold and emotionless most of the time. Life had not been roses and sunshine for him and his brothers, even if they'd had everything they asked for. They hadn't had what they needed most and that was obvious to Kane now.

His need to provide for his child, to take care of the

baby and its mother was overwhelming and almost drove him to his knees sometimes. He knew Damesha's current illness was nothing more than nerves and her pregnancy; time would heal her and make her whole again. He just hoped she'd forgive him for the things he was about to have to do.

11

---

*D*amesha woke up the next day with a foggy memory of the events of the last forty-eight hours. She wasn't sure what had been real and what had been a part of the dreams she'd been having. Did they have a Chihuahua now? Pushing her hair into a bun she wandered into the bathroom to prepare for the day. At least the nausea was gone.

She brushed her teeth and dressed, heading down to make breakfast. Kane was still asleep and though she wanted to feel peeved at him she knew he'd catered to her every need the day before. Deciding she needed the same cure she used for a hangover, she headed down to the kitchen for some orange juice and breakfast. She wasn't sure what she could take while she was pregnant so she left the medicine off of the menu. She made a note to find an OB/GYN in her area, and started breakfast.

Kane came down happy and charming as usual. He hugged her from behind, pressing into every inch of skin he could.

"I'm glad to see you up, baby. Feel better?" His words soothed her, his voice a balm rather than the irritant it had been yesterday.

She let herself relax against his body for a moment but moved as she felt Annie wiggling at her knees.

"Yes, I do. And I think Missy wants feeding. Can you do that?"

"Sure. Uh, I guess she'll be going out with me today. Do you mind?" Kane tiptoed around the question, concerned she might still be in the same bad mood she'd been in yesterday. She'd yelled at him for taking Annie downstairs with him when he'd brought her dinner last night. She'd wanted to cuddle, apparently.

"That's fine, babe. Whatever she wants to do. Who's mommy's sweet girl?" Damesha bent down to pet the dog, which gave her cheek a swipe, but ran away as she heard the bag of dog food crinkling. Damesha laughed and washed her hands before plating up pancakes and sausage.

"You, uh, sure you don't want me to spend the day at home?" Kane asked after breakfast. He was helping

Damesha wash up the dishes and pulled her to him once more. His warm breath caressed the nape of her neck as he pulled her back to his front. She shivered in his arms, desire suddenly burning through her.

Damesha knew she loved Kane and she knew things were weird at the moment but who else should she be taking solace in at the moment? She remembered how nasty she'd been with him the day before, and the anger and resentment that had caused it, but now she felt deflated and wanted her normal life back. Sure, she could call Erika in New York, cry her heart out, maybe even talk about running back home, but that's not what she wanted. Kane was what she wanted.

Turning her head, she sighed as Kane's hands came to her breasts, cupping the tender globes in his hands. Gently he found her nipples through the thin cotton of her nightgown and teased them into stiff peaks. A longer sigh escaped her lips, her head going back to lean on his shoulder.

Kane's lips burned down the long, dark trail of her neck, to the spot where her neck and shoulder met. Damesha heard him give a groan of triumph as her sighs turned to a low growl deep in her throat. Her hips pushed back against him, teasing him, teasing herself as she felt him harden against her bottom. She needed him, needed to be his.

"I'm not going anywhere just yet. Somebody needs some attention!" Kane turned her in his arms, backing her up against the counter. She braced herself, wondering exactly what he had in mind. Kane's hands moved down her body, tracing a path of heat down her sides. His body moved with his hands until he was kneeling on the floor, pushing up her nightgown.

"Oh my." Damesha breathed, her excitement rising as Kane pressed his face to her lower abdomen. His hands cupped at her stomach and she inhaled sharply. His thumbs weren't staying put, rather, they were exploring the heat between her firm thighs, seeking out her hidden depths.

Damesha watched as his tongue stroked at her folds, and desire burned hotter in her veins. When he pushed at her outer leg, she moved to give him better access to her. Pressing her open with a grunt of satisfaction, Kane dived into Demesha's sex, driving her mad with hot, wet, tiny circles that traveled up her crevice until he found the spot that made her clench his hair in her hand.

Kane's tongue stroked Damesha's clit, exciting her, then making her moan as he flattened out the organ and laved at her swollen bud. With slow, languid strokes he tormented her, holding her prisoner between desire and completion. Damesha squirmed, needing release, her body yearning for the explosion of pulsing muscles and quivering flesh that came with orgasm. But Kane prolonged her torture, keeping her in limbo as her hips thrust into his face, her cries of pleasure padded by her thighs.

"Please, Kane, please. Baby please, just let me come." Damesha's words were a plea, almost a sob as she shuddered there at the counter, her foot still braced against the handle of a drawer. "Please, baby."

Kane gave a chuckle of satisfaction, of domination, and he finally gave her what she craved the most. He turned her once more and Damesha braced herself on the counter, her right leg going up this time to give him better access to her. She could feel him behind her, tall, strong, and hot. She waited for his penetration, waited to feel that first hint of his invasion as he slid between her nether lips and when it finally came, when she felt the wide tip pressing into her, she gave in to her desire to scream.

It was a shout really, a triumphant noise of satisfaction that ended when he bottomed out inside her honeyed heat, unable to press any further into her. Kane's hand moved around, between the front of her thighs, sliding into the slick depths of her folds. He found her clit and his fingers pressed into the nub, finally sending her into the oblivion she sought.

Kane thrust into her slow and hard, hitting all the right places, but she needed more. As the spasms bloomed inside her, sending her into a land of release and oblivion, she needed more, and pressed back against him, her cries one long stream of pleasure. Damesha could feel Kane, long and hard inside her and she didn't care about anything else in that moment. All that mattered was the slide and pull of his cock inside her walls, stroking every inch of her.

The pleasure didn't end. It kept building and boiling over with each stroke of Kane's length. Damesha tried to signal that his fingers were too much on her overly sensitive clitoris, but he ignored her, and kept driving her deeper into the well of darkness that was her pleasure. When she could endure no more, when she hung limply from the counter, her body replete, she felt the pulsing explosion of Kane's release. Only when he'd given her everything she could take did he allow himself release. She gave a faint smile as Kane groaned a guttural cry of pleasure behind her.

Their bodies sank together, Kane bracing himself on his hands so he wouldn't crush Damesha as he kissed each bit of her flesh he could see. They caught their breath, ragged gasps turning to even breathing and sighs. Damesha reveled in Kane surrounding her, loving her, and keeping her safe.

"Shall I stay home today, my love?" He whispered the words into her hair, his warm breath sending shivers down her spine.

"I don't know, your hip is still healing. Maybe we should wait for round two." She pushed up, needing to stand.

Kane moved away and pulled his pants back on. She hadn't even realized he'd taken them off. Funny how you didn't notice things in the heat of the moment. Straightening, she looked over at Kane with a smile.

"How is it today? Let me see it." She moved to him, pulling at his shirt.

"It's good, I can take care of it from now on." He moved back, stepping away from seeking hands. "I'd best get to going then. I'll see you at lunch time, probably. Annie, you coming girl?" Kane stepped to the back door, taking his keys from a hook on the wall as Annie came bounding into the room once more. The humans had been making puppies so she'd wandered off.

Damesha smiled as Kane and Annie left but the smile melted away as she realized he'd not wanted her to have a look at his wound. Why? Dismissing her suspicions as silly, Damesha went into her office and opened her laptop. A quick shower and she'd get back on her project.

The hours passed quietly, but around eleven o'clock

she heard the sound of an elephant trumpeting in the woods behind the house. Damesha's calm never cracked, she simply found a streaming music service on her laptop and turned the music up. It didn't exist if she didn't hear it. With a tight smile, she went back to typing and lost herself in the project until Kane and Annie came in for lunch.

Kane was making himself a sandwich, tossing pieces of ham and cheese down to Annie who made them disappear quickly, when Damesha walked into the kitchen. He gave her a bear hug and went back to his sandwich making.

"Want a sandwich darling?" he asked absently as he fed Annie another piece of ham.

"No wonder she likes you more, you feed her constantly." Damesha pulled bottles of juice from the fridge and some chips from a cabinet before setting them on the table. "And yes, if you can spare a piece of ham, I'll have a sandwich."

"You need to spend less time in that office and more time outdoors. Get some air. Why don't you come riding with me this afternoon?" He put the sandwiches on a plate and sat at the table with her.

"I might, you know. I haven't been anywhere since I got back. I'm getting tired of staring at the same walls. Yeah, I will go with you." She ran upstairs to get dressed and came back down to see Annie looking rather dejected.

"Oh baby, we'll be back before you know it. You can chase off any scary monsters that might come around." Annie gave Damesha a doubtful look and put her head back on her paws. "That little face, oh you know how to give a guilt trip!"

Damesha got down on the floor to love on Annie for a moment, the dog swiping her nose with adoration and forgiveness before Damesha stood back up.

"She'll be fine, Damesha. She can get out, she has food and water. She'll be fine." Kane went to the back door and took down his keys again. Kane was a creature of habit when it came to some things. Damesha pushed the thoughts away that threatened to intrude on her tranquillity and followed Kane out of the door. It was time to see where they lived.

They rode for hours, Kane stopping twice to check some fencing that had fallen or been pushed down by animals scratching themselves on the barbed wire. Damesha tried not to let her thoughts wander too much, tried to stay focused on the ride and the scenery but things wanted to intrude.

When she thought she heard a lion's roar she blocked it out. When she could have sworn she'd seen a chimpanzee hanging from a tree, she turned her head away.

When her hands tightened around Kane's waist when one of the quad bike's tires found a hole and he didn't even gasp, she put it off to good genes. Nothing was wrong.

But when she got off the bike to answer the call of nature and found that, suddenly, her stomach was in the way of her resting right up against Kane's back she knew she couldn't pretend that everything was normal, All-American-Apple-Pie-and-Fireworks-normal anymore. Something strange was happening. Something very odd was going on and this wasn't how things were supposed to be going. How had her stomach come out that far in a few minutes? And how was she going to tell Kane?

Damesha grew quieter as the day progressed, her breasts suddenly more sore, her back aching, and she felt something...odd. She wasn't sure what but she almost felt as though there was, well, someone listening to her. She looked around but couldn't see anyone. She knew the sensation was coming from inside of her. This wasn't a movie though, this was her life, and she knew babies couldn't communicate with their mothers before birth. It was impossible. The thought was also kind of creepy, what if the baby had been listening earlier?

Telling herself to chill out, Damesha went into the house and began to prepare dinner while Kane showered. She ran into the small bathroom downstairs for a shower of her own and came out even more puzzled. The stomach that had been only slightly rounded this morning was most definitely protruding and her breasts wouldn't fit into her bra. Her panties had stretched over her hips far more than the last time she wore the fresh pair. Her dress, loose fitting and comfortable was now tight on the arms and did little to hide her stomach.

Damesha left the bra in the bathroom, along with the panties, and pulled the dress on. Kane came down to join her and his hands slid over the bulge of her stomach but he didn't say a word. She'd frozen as his hands moved but somehow he hadn't noticed. Men could be so very unobservant sometimes! Damesha was almost miffed that Kane hadn't noticed her tummy but pulled the chicken casserole she'd prepared out of the oven along with some rolls.

Kane didn't seem to notice anything odd about her and carried on the conversation as though it was a normal day. Damesha just picked at her food at first but started to eat quickly after the first couple of bites. She became ravenously hungry as the food touched her tongue. She forgot Kane was there, or Annie at her feet under the table hoping for a dropped morsel. All she could do was eat until half of the casserole was gone. The dish should have fed six people!

She looked up guiltily as she realized what she'd just done. Kane gave her a smile and went to the fridge for a beer. Damesha excused herself, shocked at how much she'd just eaten. Right, she was going back to New York, back to sanity. She'd call Erika and get her to arrange a doctor appointment, there had to be a way to fix this. She'd come home after that and life would go on. Nothing to see, nothing to report. She hoped.

"There's something wrong with me. I think I'm losing my mind. You see what I just did right?" She'd consumed the food like a starving person offered a buffet!

"Damesha, baby, you're fine, I promise. Sometimes people get these kind of growth spurts where their bodies crave more food, that's all." He sounded as though he was trying to convince them both.

Damesha started to protest, to start to list off all of the things that had happened so far, but he got a phone call from his brother. Damesha could only sigh as he kissed her goodbye before going to answer his brother's summons. Duty called, but not his duty to her.

She cleaned up the dishes and was about to watch television when the doorbell rang. She went into the front of the house to answer the door but there was no one there. The sun was just going down and she could still see out of the window, there wasn't anyone there.

Damesha shrugged it off as a malfunction in the doorbell when she heard a knock on the back door. Now that definitely came from a human hand! She went back into the kitchen but once more, there wasn't anyone there. Damesha felt all of the hairs on her skin as they all stood on end. Something weird was happening again.

She locked the doors and made sure all of the windows were locked. She went upstairs and locked herself in the bedroom. She could hear howls in the woods and strange noises. It sounded like an entire zoo was trampling through the yard. The sun had retreated now and it was full dark out, the moon barely a sliver in the sky. The flood lights weren't on either, she'd forgotten to turn them on!

A multitude of hands slapping against glass, doors, the very walls, left her screaming as terror filled her, gripping her throat as the hand drummed a rhythmic beat against the house. It sounded as though a hundred hands were beating against the house, a slapping sound that reminded her of batons striking plastic shields. Damesha ran into the bathroom, trying to call Kane with her mobile phone. Her shaking fingers swiped the wrong name several times before she found Kane's.

"Hello...Kane!" she started, but stopped as she realized the call had gone to voicemail. Why wasn't he answering the phone?

She hunkered down in the shower, wondering if she should call the police when she remembered the attitude of the cop she'd met already. Sheriff, deputy, whatever he was. She'd dismissed him from her mind until now. He was probably the one they'd send out and with her luck, he'd call ahead and ask the people outside if he could bring some gasoline to the party. No, she couldn't call him. Terrified, Damesha huddled in the tub, her hands over her ears to block out the racket.

Annie, she thought suddenly. Where is Annie? Damesha felt her panic ease as she remembered Annie had followed along Kane when he left earlier. That minute adjustment of panic was soon increased as howls, screams, and other noises joined into the cacophony taking place outside. Damesha huddled in the tub, whimpering, helpless as the noises continued outside. With her eyes closed to the world and her hands over her ears, Damesha retreated into a dream world, a world that existed only in her head.

Kane was there, as was their child, a girl, small and tiny, her chubby fists waving as her parents pulled her into the water, allowing her to float on her back, her mother's secure hand beneath her bottom. Damesha held the girl so her back was in the water and she watched as her daughter's little arms and legs kicked in glee. Then her daughter suddenly morphed into a seal and swam away. Damesha screamed in horror at her child transforming into an animal and swum away. She stood screaming for her child to come back as she sank into the water, reaching for her little girl.

12

Kane strode into his brother's office and flung the door open without worrying about whether the door knob would scuff the wall or not. He'd had about enough of this being summoned bullshit. He was a grown man and his brother wasn't his master. Well, he kind of was, but that wasn't the point. The point was everybody else in their clan had free choice, why couldn't he?

Just because his chosen mate was a human didn't mean he should be treated any differently, or that she should be treated any differently. Kane's anger had grown as he'd drove to his brother's house. Cade was always interrupting him, barging into his life lately, and this was the last time.

Damesha wasn't doing well, he wasn't exactly sure

why but he knew his clan was responsible for the how. She was in for a shock anyway, Kane and his clan weren't normal human beings, they were shifters, able to shift into any creature they desired. There was always one creature that was easier to shift into than others, one that the shifter felt the most at home in, but they could usually shift into whatever they chose.

Unfortunately, Damesha had already witnessed what happens when a shifter is injured and starts to lose control of their shifting. That little Chihuahua she'd had a run-in with was him. After his injury, he'd healed quickly, far too quickly to escape her notice, and had been unable to control the shifting. This uncontrolled shifting had been the reason he'd started going out so much, so she wouldn't see him shift or what he'd turn into.

That had been one of the most humiliating moments of his life. Not only had she seen him as a tiny defenseless animal, even if she hadn't known it was him, she'd had to take him outside to use the bathroom. If humiliated anger had been enough to make him shift he'd have been a human in less than a millisecond but nothing would make him shift when he was that weakened except his body's will. For whatever reason it had wanted to be a cute little puppy at that point; probably an effort to comfort Damesha.

Often, Kane had wanted to tell Damesha the truth, to bring her into his world, but he was forbidden. Revealing your true nature to a non-shifter was punishable by death, for a multitude of reasons, mainly that it put the whole shifter-verse into danger if it was revealed. That was if anyone believed them in the first place.

Kane strode into Cade's office with this thought in mind. He had to reveal the truth to Damesha, she thought she was losing her mind and it was starting to show. The poor woman was a far cry from the brave, independent soul he'd fallen in love with. Now she was frightened of her own shadow and though she tried to put a brave face on it, she looked haunted.

"Kane, glad you could grace me with your presence." Cade's sarcastic tone wasn't lost on Kane.

"Well, to be honest, I'd rather tell you to go fuck yourself, but all of these little chats we're having lately, I guess you must really love me brother dear." Kane fluttered his eyelids at his brother before taking a seat. Annie had followed him inside and sat daintily at his side, her warm brown eyes looking in Cade's direction with disdain. Kane almost laughed when he saw the expression on the dog's face; Annie was funny like that.

"I guess it's getting tedious but so is your fascination

with this woman. It's time you dealt with it and got rid of her!" Cade's fist came down on his desk.

Kane watched his brother, noting the tight jaw, the narrowed eyes, and grim line of his mouth. Cade was at the end of his patience but so was Kane. Cade thought Kane could just turn his emotions off, and send Damesha on her way.

"My spirit has chosen her Cade. How many times do I have to tell you? We both know what happens when a shifter is denied their mate. I'll die without her." Kane shot his brother a glance of consternation. It was common lore amongst their kind. The only way a shifter could be separated from their chosen mate without facing death themselves was through the death of the mate. That death released the spirit to find another mate or to live out their lives.

"Fuck off, Kane, that's just an old wives' tale! There's no such thing as mating for life. Don't be so ridiculous." Cade's dismissive tone came with a wave of his hand, a gesture that pissed Kane off.

"Really? Then what happened to our parents then? They just died of…what?" Kane looked at his brother with disgust. "Kept in perfectly good environments, fed, and cared for by the Mungon clan, they just died of nothing? You really believe that?"

Cade's face tensed even more at the mention of the

Mungon and his words came out as hard little points. "The Mungon tortured our parents, kept them in damp cells, denied them food and water..."

"Come off it, Cade, you aren't still buying Jadrian's theory on how they died, are you? The Mungon kept our parents to try to force their hands, to force the hands of all of the shifter world, into revealing our true natures. They kept them separate because, unlike you, they believed the mating would do its magic and our parents would give in to their demands before death took them. They died rather than telling the secret but you just want to believe the Mungon's tortured them!"

"You're the baby of the family, you weren't even old enough to remember them. How can you know what truly happened? No, we aren't going into this decade's long war with the Mungon. We're going to deal with that troublesome group and their "motorcycle club" before it's over with. We're talking about you and that *woman.* I know she stood by you at the hospital and I know she took care of you when you were released, but she's *not* one of us, Kane!" Cade stood up, pacing his office. "You have to let her go. We can't let our secret get out!"

Kane glared at his brother, not sure how to make the other man see this was his life, not Cade's, and sure as fuck not the clan's. "I guess that means you won't be giving me your permission to marry her then? You know she's carrying my child, yet you'll still deny me even that?"

"Certainly not, little brother! Child or no, you won't be marrying that woman. And you know what the penalty for defying me is." Cade glared at his brother, his nostrils flared.

"I know, I know, the same as it is for everything in our world. I'll die if I defy you, I'll die if I don't stay near her, I'll die if I marry without your permission, I'll die if I tell her the truth, I'll die, I'll die, I'll die." Kane slumped in his chair, defeated for the moment.

"That's right. Don't force me to make that decision, Kane. I wouldn't want to have to call for your death, to put the clan through that, but I will if you force me to. I have to. It's my duty."

"And duty is all that matters to you, I know. Fuck your brothers, your blood, fuck your own life even, because your precious duty comes first. I know Cade." Kane stood, preparing to leave his brother's office. The office of the chief of their clan.

"One more thing, Kane. If she's not gone in the next few days, we'll take matters into our own hands." Cade spoke softly, without looking into Kane's eyes.

"Into your own…what the hell are you talking

about?" Kane turned back to Cade, his own gaze approaching fury.

"Don't force us to show you." Cade finally looked into Kane's eyes, so similar to his own. Normally Kane's were softer, but now Cade saw a fierceness in his youngest brother's eyes that he'd never seen before and it shook him. It was trouble for the whole clan, what he saw in Kane's eyes. "Don't Kane."

"Go fuck yourself, Cade." Kane shot over his shoulder, his hand going over his shoulder to flash his middle finger at his brother. "I don't take kindly to threats."

Kane left his brother's house, the clan's house, and drove back to his own. His brother had threatened his life, but more importantly, they'd threatened Damesha. That was unacceptable. Fuck him and his clan. Kane knew that meant Cade's chosen cadre of clan soldiers. It was time for a plan.

He pulled into the driveway at the house and ran through the eerily silent house.

"Damesha? Damesha where are you, baby?" Kane strode through the downstairs, Annie passing him up to run to the bedroom.

Kane didn't pay attention to Annie and kept searching through the house. He had left her office and was heading into the living room, looking for at least a note of some kind, when he heard Annie barking. Annie never barked, never, and to hear her barking now meant something.

Kane followed the sound of her barking, a frantic, terrified sound that went right through him, raising goose bumps on his entire body. Kane found Annie in the bedroom, at the bathroom door, her nails clawing long scratches in the wood as she tried to get through the door. Kane knew something was wrong then, Annie didn't act like this.

His hand shook as he reached for the knob, he was terrified of what he was going to find. A lot of bad things happened in bathrooms, things with razors and blood that he didn't want to think about. Surely it hadn't gotten to that point yet?

Kane threw the door open and Annie raced in, heading straight for the tub hidden behind a shower curtain. He heard a startled sound as she jumped right into the tub, clearing the edge easily, but ignored the curtain. Whoever Annie was on, licking at frantically, was now covered in the shower curtain pulled from its clips.

"Damesha?" Kane knelt in front of the tub, pulling the curtain away to reveal the woman he loved. She was there, huddled in the tub, her hands over her ears, her eyes squeezed shut, strange mewling noises coming from her throat as Annie continued to frantically lick at her mistress.

"Annie, get down darling, let's get her out of here." Kane eased Annie away but the dog went back to Damesha, her nose digging at the space between Damesha's head and the tub, trying to encourage her mistress to get up.

Kane pulled Annie away and grabbed at Damesha, pulling her out of the tub. He didn't know what had happened but he knew enough was enough. Somehow his family had caused this, he knew it after that warning from Cade. This was his brother's doing.

Kane carried Damesha into the bedroom and put her down on the bed. He pulled away her clothes and put a fresh nightgown on her trembling frame. He tried to cover her but Annie jumped on top of the cover.

"No, Annie, you can get under the cover with her but not sit on top of it like that, you'll make her uncomfortable." Kane held up the comforter and Annie bounced beneath the cover, straight beside Damesha's body. Kane could see Annie was pressing herself into the still trembling woman's back. She would keep Damesha warm and safe.

Kane ran downstairs to make some chamomile tea and rushed back up with it. Neither Damesha nor the dog had moved. Annie was pressed into Damesha's back, Damesha on her side with her legs pulled up to her abdomen. Damesha still wouldn't speak, her eyes staring into the darkness, and Kane felt helpless. How did he fix this?

He put the cup of tea down and moved to sit in front of Damesha, pulling her into his arms. Annie protested with a fussing noise, but settled back against Damesha's hips without further protest. Kane started talking to Damesha, hoping he could sooth the obvious terror that had caused this. He didn't know what that terror had been but he knew she hadn't deserved it.

"It's alright, baby, I'm here now. I'm never going to leave you alone here again. Come on now, you're safe." Kane started to rock the woman he loved, hoping it would soothe her. He knew she wasn't a baby but the motion worked for a reason. He heard her start to snore slight little sounds, and sighed in relief. Sleep would be good for her.

He looked down. Her hair was wild, eyes sunken even in sleep, and knew she'd been terrified. She didn't look injured, not physically anyway, and the baby was alright. She just needed some rest. He leaned back against the headboard and started to plan his next move. He was almost certain they were going to have to leave the town, leave Kansas, but this was the best place for her while she was pregnant. It was also the best place for her to give birth, the doctors here were all shifters, they knew what shifters needed.

He knew Damesha couldn't take much more exposure to this torment. He'd dismissed it when she'd first mentioned the animal noises, assuming she'd heard some roaming shifters in the woods. They often came to the family's woods to run free for a while. He'd been startled when she first mentioned it but had quickly written it off. Now he wasn't so certain the acts hadn't been malicious.

He'd gaslighted her a bit over that whole Chihuahua business, making himself feel like a total heel, but he couldn't tell her the truth. Instead, he'd pretended the whole night hadn't happened, that she'd imagined it. He'd been able to communicate with Annie in the dog form and she'd gone out to keep an eye out for trouble until he could shift back to a human. Kane knew that night played a part in Damesha's break with reality and wanted to take a whip to himself. His life depended on him keeping the truth to himself, he couldn't tell her.

Not that the clan would know if he did, not unless she let slip that she knew about them. That would earn them both a quick death. Kane trusted her, knew that she wouldn't tell the world about the shifter communities amongst the "normal" human communities, but she might let slip to someone in the clan that she knew about them and that could be dangerous.

"How am I going to explain about the baby, Annie? It could be a shifter." Kane spoke out loud to the dog, but only got a moaning sound from the dog. "That's not much help. I don't know what Cade thinks is going to happen when Damesha has this baby and it decides to turn into a parrot or a water buffalo and she freaks out. I don't think he's totally thought this through."

Annie's only response was to wave her head around under the covers before settling back into her place. Obviously, she had no clue what Cade had planned either and didn't care, her mistress needed her. Kane thought Annie's response a bit dismissive and decided maybe she was right to be. It was his fault Damesha was in this mess. He should have been more careful.

"I wasn't thinking, Annie. I was falling in love for the first time in my life. I was a little selfish, wasn't I?" Annie made a noise of agreement.

Shifter's didn't catch diseases like non-humans did. They were immune to all of them. Injuries could harm them but sicknesses were usually of a shifter-kind, not something non-shifter humans spread around. That didn't mean they couldn't get those same humans pregnant. Essentially shifters were human, there was just a slight difference in their makeup, a magic that was missing in normal humans.

How was he going to explain all this to her? Kane knew she'd run screaming, ready to have him locked up in a loony bin if he told her without shifting. That might still make her run screaming though.

He decided there wasn't much he could do tonight and he only had a short time to spare. In the morning he'd pack up some of their things, take out the bundle that contained half his inheritance from his parents in cash, and they'd make a run for an island with no links to the outside world. That should keep them safe. Damesha wouldn't like it but it had to be done if they wanted to stay together. He'd figure out the rest along the way.

Kane settled into the bed, a plan of some sort finally in place, and a direction to head in decided. He could rest now, even if he only half slept, his ears still listening for any signs of danger.

13

Kane woke the next morning and found Damesha sitting on the edge of their bed. Her stomach was more noticeable now and her breasts were larger. Her eyes still held that dull, lost look and he felt his heart tearing in two. He'd caused that look, whether he'd done everything that brought her to this moment or not. He'd done this to her.

Kane's alpha side, the side that growled down a cop on the day they met, that stood up to his brother, that helped him through a crash that should have killed him, finally kicked into gear and he stood up. He undressed, cleaned his teeth and face, and came back into the room. Damesha was still sitting on the bed.

"Right, this could cost me my life, maybe even yours, but I can't let this go any further. Damesha." He looked over at her but she was still staring at the walls. *"Damesha!"*

Her dull eyes turned in his direction but he knew she didn't see him. With a huge sigh he shouted her name once more. He saw a spark of something, anger, annoyance, in her eyes and smiled. He was getting somewhere now. Then he shifted.

Before her eyes, Kane suddenly turned into a gorilla. This was Kane's natural form, the form that was most comfortable to him. He was short and stocky, covered in black fur. A massive specimen of the species. Kane was ferocious in this form and capable of many things, mainly bad things. This was the shift Kane had the most trouble with because it was hard to control his temper, his instincts, in this shifter shape. This was his demon form, his killer form.

Damesha stared dumbly at him, and Kane felt defeat creeping in once more. He couldn't speak to her in this form but he could have found a way to communicate with her. Making a growling noise he prepared to shift again, into something bigger maybe. A scream from the bed changed his mind.

Kane saw her scrabbling across the bed, awareness and terror in her eyes. He was glad about the awareness but felt terrible for the terror. He moved closer to the bed, his hand out to her, and made a sound of supplication. She jumped over the side of the bed, only her forehead and her terribly blue eyes, the eyes he adored, showing now.

"What the hell?" she said.

He came to the edge of the bed, his head still reaching over the mattress despite the frame's height.

He reached out his arm as far as it would go and made another sound as he put his head down on the bed. He was submitting to her and hoped she recognized it. He saw the war within her mind displayed across her face, fear turned to uncertainty, and that turned into curiosity. Damesha held out her own hand finally and just as she grasped his warm, leathery fingers he shifted back into himself.

She shouted once more and threw herself back against the wall, ending up on her bottom as she stared up at him.

"Oh my God, Kane. I've lost my mind! I could have sworn you were just a gorilla!" Her pulse was racing in her neck, he could see it beating frantically in the hollow beneath her jaw.

"No baby, you aren't crazy. Here, I'll do it again." This time he shifted into the Chihuahua she'd seen him as before and toddled over to her.

He jumped onto her thigh and scrabbled up her chest to lick her jaw before he hopped down once more. She looked down at the tiny dog and Kane knew she understood now. And she wasn't running. That was a good sign.

Shifting back to himself he looked up at her.

"Does it all make sense now?" He hoped she'd forgive him.

"No, not really. But yeah, I guess it does. You've had a secret. I can either take that as you making a fool out of me or as you had a secret to keep. Which was it?" She sounded like she wanted to be angry but couldn't quite get there.

"It's a secret baby, one I'm not allowed to tell a normal person. Ever. It could mean we both die if the clan ever finds out. I couldn't let this go on. Not with the baby, not with you thinking you were losing your mind."

"Right." Damesha's lost gaze was now a stunned display of her inner thoughts, not a lost woman with no way back to reality.

"It's going to take some getting used to. I have a plan. I don't know if you'll like it but it'll keep us both safe. You have to pay attention now, baby. I know this is a lot to take in but we have to act quickly. We're going to get dressed and act like we're just going out of town for the day, that's all. We'll have to leave most things behind but you can bring your work stuff. We'll figure out how to disable tracking and all of that." Too late Kane realized his plan was far more complicated than he'd originally thought. She wouldn't leave without her phone, her laptop, or her tablet. Those could all be used to track them.

"Actually, I've emailed all of the files to a private cloud, it can't be traced. We can leave all of that of too." Kane looked at her in shock. She still looked dazed but her words were calm, rational, and right there with him.

She turned to face him finally, her head coming up from its position of staring at the floor.

"Whatever it takes, baby. You made me a promise for life. I never gave you that same promise but I meant to. For life." Her gaze was intense, fierce, and full of the love she felt for him. But still no mention of the baby; that hurt him a little. It was an awkward time though. She had a good reason for keeping quiet. "I kind of liked how your eyes turned orange there, by the way."

He laughed ruefully as she stood up, brushing her hair behind her ears. He gave her one of those slow sexy grins she loved so much and she embraced him. For a moment she shuddered against him, the last remnants of her terror, but he knew she was waking up now. His Damesha was back.

"Get a shower, Mesha, then let's get gone." He kissed the side of her head, loving the feel of her in his arms.

This was worth giving up everything. This was all he needed.

She let him go and went into the bathroom. She showered quickly and found the few things Annie would need. She came to him after packing everything in her large handbag, a small dark blue book in her hand.

"Do I need my passport?" He hadn't told her where they were going yet.

"You might, let me grab mine." Kane ran to his own office and came back quickly. "Right then, let's blow this popsicle stand."

"What does that even mean? I've never seen a popsicle stand, have you?" Damesha wondered as they left the house, not even looking back as they went to his new truck, a much more modern version of his old one but somehow without the mystique of the old one.

"I have no idea but we're going to do it. Annie, you ready girl?" Kane looked down at Annie who swiped his nose with her soft tongue. "I'll take that as a yes. Let's get going then."

Kane drove for hours, heading south, taking them through a small portion of Oklahoma before they made it into Texas. They didn't speak a lot, Kane driving and Damesha pondering what the hell she'd just learned.

She'd ask him a question every now and then and go back to pondering.

"Does it hurt?" she'd asked earlier.

"No," he'd told her with honesty. "It's more like a pop then you're something else."

"Oh." She'd gone quiet but spoke up a half hour later.

"Do you think like a human?"

"Not always. Sometimes nature takes over in the heat of the moment and you think like that animal would."

"Is that frightening?" She didn't look at him, just stared out of the window beside of her head.

"It can be, when you shift back. Knowing the animal instinct took over can be disconcerting."

"Right." Her jaw twisted for a minute as though she were chewing something and she went quiet again.

"Does this mean you're way older than you say you are?" She'd finally turned to him and her gaze was open, curious.

"Not me, no. Some shifters are, but I'm the age I say I am. We all get different gifts, I guess you can call them, but mine isn't slow aging."

"I see. What is your gift?"

"I haven't found out yet. It's like that sometimes. Some of us never find out." He dismissed the question, he wasn't worried about gifts, just life.

"Can we stop for food? It's been a while." She asked it

in the same tone as her other questions, not flat, but not excited.

"Oh, sure, baby, sorry." He pulled off an exit with a sign full of restaurants, pulling into the one she asked for.

Kane had planned on leaving the restaurant and traveling deeper into Texas but Damesha changed that plan. To their server's amazement, Damesha ordered three starters, two full meals, and three desserts. And ate every bite of them. Kane hadn't expected it but knew that expectant shifter mothers could consume a great deal of food. He had to tamp down his thoughts as the server came back and asked them if they needed anything else. Kane wasn't surprised when Damesha ordered a chili dog. Damesha wolfed that down quickly and they finally left the restaurant, Damesha a little food drunk.

"I can't believe I just ate all of that." She sounded sleepy and Kane took Annie for her walk as Damesha climbed back into the truck. When he came back she was asleep.

He saw a sign for a hotel up the street and pulled in, paying for their room as he'd done with the food; in cash. He'd left his cards in the glove box of the truck to keep temptation away. He didn't want to be tracked. He woke Damesha up when they got to their room and helped her into the room. She fell into the bed, asleep before her head hit the pillow. He didn't think she was going to be pregnant too much longer at this rate. Shifter pregnancies didn't last as long as non-shifter pregnancies.

Annie had one more walk after a bowl of water and food, and settled in between Damesha and Kane. Kane quickly fell asleep too, the day of driving mixed with the stress to make him tired. His breathing settled and the room went quiet as all three finally got some much needed peaceful rest.

"KANE, *Kane!!* Kane, wake up honey. We have to go back." Damesha's voice pulled him from a dream where they sat on white sandy beaches, Annie chasing the surf. The cool air in the room made him pull the covers over his head as he turned over. "No, Kane, wake up!"

Damesha pulled the covers away from him and he sat up, suddenly awake.

"What's wrong?" He looked around, his ears tuned in for danger but nothing seemed to be wrong.

"We have to go back. Now. Tonight." Her face was a mask of worry and he glanced at the clock.

"Baby, it's one in the morning, can't it wait?" He sat back in bed, his body crying out for more sleep.

"No, your brother is in danger. Jadrian? I never did learn the others names, only Cade. But Jadrian, he's adopted right? He's in trouble." She wouldn't look him in the eye.

"How do you know that?" He'd heard psychics existed but had never met one. It seemed Damesha had more secrets than she'd told him.

"I, well, I just know things sometimes. You know how I trusted you over this shifter thing? Well, you have to trust me on this. He's in a whole lot of danger. I've never been able to stop something from happening before but I've never really tried. Are there really vampires? And can their blood really get you high? Wouldn't it just, I don't know, turn you or whatever?" She looked at him askance, her voice revealing her amazement.

"Yeah, there are. There's a whole slew of things that are real that the world plays off as fake. And yes, vampire blood really will get you high. High as a kite. It especially works on shifters. And no, it won't turn you. So what's Jadrian's issue?" Kane was putting his clothes back on.

"Seems he's tangled up with some vampires, some that sell their blood. He's been trying to get rid of them, they're starting to sell it in your area now." Damesha didn't have to finish, he knew where this was heading. Vampires weren't to be fucked with, but Jadrian thought he was some kind of knight in shining armor, there to act as the world's savior.

"Let's go." Kane's exhaustion had left him. "When is this going to happen?"

"A few days from now. We have time, but we need to get back. I saw Cade being distracted because he'd found us. If we don't get back your brother will be too busy looking for us to see what's going on with Jadrian."

"After all they've done to you, Damesha, you're still trying to protect them?" They were all in the truck now, traveling again.

"They're your brothers, your clan, your people. I can't let this happen. If we're there it'll change something anyway." Damesha cuddled Annie close. "Besides, you could hate me forever if I let it happen."

"I'd totally understand, actually, but it would hurt yes. Get some rest baby, put the seat back." He brushed at her soft hair, pushing it out of her light blue eyes. "We'll be home soon enough."

Kane drove through the darkness, his concern growing with each mile. Jadrian was a big boy but the vampires weren't to be messed with. Inviting them into their ongoing war with the Mungons was just stupid. It would split the defenses of Cade's cadre of soldiers. It might be even more stupid than Kane running away.

He knew what it took for Damesha to say those words to him and respected her greatly for it. Whether Kane would or not was going to be another matter. But he'd find a way to make Cade see. He had to.

14

$\mathcal{K}$ane drove straight to Cade's house, not caring what time it was, or if his brother might still be asleep, he needed to know what was happening. Kane marched into the house, and went to his brother's room.

"Wake up, Cade." For once Kane was happy about having free rein through the house, it meant he didn't have to deal with his brother's soldiers. "Wake up, Cade!"

It came out louder the second time. Cade was awake and on his feet in an instant.

"What's wrong?" Cade blinked for a moment then sat back down.

"Jadrian's in some serious shit, about to start a war we can't afford." Kane sat down beside his brother.

"What are you talking about?" Cade scrubbed at his eyes before looking at Kane again.

"He's mixed up with some Phlebos." Phlebos was the term used in the magical world for vampires that sold their own blood. Phlebotomists, Phelbos for short.

"Fuck." Kane heard Cade swear under his breath.

"Yep. And it's not going to end well. Begin well, whatever."

"Jadrian's going to die?" Cade's head snapped in Kane's direction. They all knew Jadrian was Cade's favorite brother. They were the same age and despite being adopted they were eerily similar.

"Yes." Kane's word cam out bluntly, without emotion. Jadrian was too much like Cade, but he loved him. He loved all of his brothers, even if they acted like dicks.

"Which psychic told you this?" Cade assumed that's how Kane found out.

"Not one of ours," Kane said carefully, not sure how, or whether he should, reveal that Damesha was the source.

"Who then?" Cade demanded, his voice starting to rise. "I need to question them."

"Damesha," Kane said her name quietly. She was sitting downstairs with Annie, safe in the house.

"Damesha? Your little human woman? She's psychic.

Fuck that means she knows about us then. Probably always has." Cade's voice sounded worried.

"I think she probably has yes. But she came to me with this information, she didn't run off and tell the papers, or sell her story." Kane played along with Cade's theory, seeing a way out of the death punishment for them both.

"Well, not much we can do about that, now is there? Right then, bring her in. I need to talk to her." Cade stood to dress. Kane stared at his brother. "Well? Go on then."

"You were threatening her life yesterday, now you want me to bring her to you?"

"That's obviously changed now, hasn't it, little brother? She's shown her loyalty. As one of the "others" as some like to call our kind, she has her own secrets to keep anyway. Bring her up, she's safe."

Just like that, the worry, stress, plans to run away and plot to make Cade see things his way, all became pointless. Damesha had been accepted into his clan. That still wasn't the same as being allowed to marry but it was a step in the right direction.

Kane brought her to his brother's office, the man already sitting at his desk. Kane had whispered to her quickly as he went to her.

"If he asks, you sensed the truth when we met, you've

always known we were shifters. It's part of your abilities."

Damesha nodded her head in agreement. "I guess I kind of knew that, really. Everything went quiet around you. Sometimes I can hear people's thoughts, it can get noisy. But around you, I can't even hear the slight buzz that seems to permeate everything. I'd never noticed it until it was gone."

Kane was surprised but held his tongue as they entered his brother's office. That could be useful, if she knew how to control it. Obviously, she'd not been trained properly. He could rectify that with a phone call.

"Thank you for coming to us with this information, Damesha. I'd like to ask you a few things, if you don't mind?" Cade's gaze was softer, gentler, as he looked at her.

"Oh, no, it's cool." Kane knew she was nervous and squeezed her hand.

"Do you know where this even takes place?"

Cade spent thirty minutes probing her memory, and they figured out the location and a date. Damesha saw Jadrian in an office with a digital clock on the wall.

Kane was allowed to take her home after that, with a warning to take care of her. Cade's entire demeanor had changed in a matter of moments. Kane's head was spinning with it all but Damesha wasn't done for the night.

"Kane, I need to tell you something. I'm guessing you may have already figured it out. I mean, I'm as big as a house now, look at me." Damesha pointed to her bulging stomach, much bigger than it had been the day before.

"Tell me," he urged, wanting to have that moment, that moment where she finally told him.

"I'm going to have a baby. We're going to be parents. You're going to be a father." She smiled up at him, her strong teeth gleaming in the moonlight of their bedroom.

"Wow." He couldn't manage more than that.

"I think it talks to me too. I can hear this faint voice but it's growing stronger. Not really a voice, so much, but words. It's so weird but amazing!" Damesha pulled him to her, her excitement growing.

"That's normal with shifter pregnancies. It doesn't necessarily mean the baby is a shifter but…" His words trailed off as she froze.

"Shifter baby?" She looked up at him uncertainly.

"It's a possibility." His answer was brief; he couldn't offer any more than that.

"Oh." She pulled away, looking out of the window before coming back to him and leaping into his tired arms. "How wonderful!"

Kane laughed and carried her to the bed, her warm body wiping away even the tiniest shred of fatigue.

Desire replaced it as her lips found his, and he settled her on the bed. Their bodies fused as Kane followed her down, settling between her thighs. Her stomach got in the way so he decided kissing time was over. At least of her lips.

Kane stroked the smooth skin revealed when her loose top dragged as he slid up her body. His fingers danced over her ribs and cupped her right breast, the peak already tight and hard. With soft strokes, he made her purr, her body already on fire for him. He pressed his groin into her mons, her heat burning through his jeans to surround him.

Kane moved away, tossing his clothes to the ground before removing her knit pants and loose top. He loved the flowing clothing she wore but he preferred her naked. Especially when she was beneath him. Kane groaned as he felt himself hardening even more. He didn't think this was going to last long if he didn't control himself.

His eyes flashed orange for a moment and Damesha gasped. But he controlled himself and his eyes went back to their strange black color, full of desire for her. He came beside her, pulling her into his arms. He needed her kisses.

Their tongues danced as his fingers wound around her body, her own dancing down his side to come to rest between them. He gasped and thrust himself into her hand as her small hand wrapped around his cock, the pleasure of her smooth fingers wrapping around him almost too much.

"I love you," he gasped, reveling in her touch.

Damesha had never been timid but now her boldness grew. She pushed him back gently, her mouth going to work on his nipples. Kane had known many lovers in his lifetime, from all walks of their world, but Damesha was the only one that had ever grazed her tongue across his nipples. The sensation was incredible and he knew why women liked it.

He pressed into her hot mouth, the moist heat intoxicating as her hand found him once more. His breathing was ragged, his hips moving of their own accord in tempo with her hand, when she moved down suddenly, engulfing his engorged length in her wet mouth.

"Fuck! Damesha!" He tried to pull away but she wouldn't budge, her sucking mouth holding her in place.

Kane gave up and let her have her way. She wanted this, she could have it. He groaned again as she sucked harder, her hand going down to cup his sac. When her fingers began to gently roll the globes in her hand he lost his will to hold back and his fingers tightened in the sheets. His feet dug into the bed and his hips arched up, a frantic movement taking hold that he couldn't stop.

"Damesha." He gasped her name as the first jet of his seed left the tip of his tormented organ, and he came harder when he felt her throat muscles swallowing his offering. He pumped into her mouth as she moaned in pleasure, her own pleasure growing.

This is what true love-making was, he realized. Reveling in each other's pleasure. Giving pleasure by being pleasured. Kane's world rocked as his came, his body and mind completely engulfed by the ministrations of Damesha. This was love.

Kane's body finally relaxed as Damesha let him go, a laugh escaping him as she wiped at her mouth.

"You're beautiful. Thank you for that." He took her hand and pulled her up beside of him.

"I love doing that for you. It's exciting, watching you lose control."

"As long as that's the only way you want to watch me lose control." He chuckled trying to think of how to give back the pleasure she'd given. "Come up here."

He urged her to straddle him, his softened sex hardening again already. He never needed long.

"Oh my, ready again." Damesha had learned it never took him long but was still surprised.

"Lean forward." He steadied her for a moment until she found a balancing point and then moved his hand, pushing her swollen breasts together.

Kane swiped a tongue across her swollen nipples and her response was to grind her wet pussy across his length. Kane shifted as he began to suck at her nipples and her greedy depths instantly sucked him in. They both gave a grunt of satisfaction as his entire length disappeared inside of her and Damesha began to ride him, her hips moving languidly as he sucked at her.

Kane could feel her passion growing in how wet she became, flooding him with her moisture, and in the way her walls grasped at him, pulling him deeper. She shifted and her quiet passion turned to cries of joy as she found the perfect spot. Kane continued to suck at her nipples, licking them for emphasis. When he bit them gently, she pressed them deeper into his mouth.

"More," she demanded. Her inhaled breath sounded icy cold as it hissed between her teeth but she demanded even more. "Harder!"

Her fingers were buried in his hair, her hips writhing over him, driving him as he bit once more into the tender flesh. She was definitely becoming a shifter mate now.

Kane tried to distract himself from an impending orgasm by thinking about the possibilities. Damesha could become a shifter once she gave birth to their child, the mingling of blood causing the spontaneous conversion. This didn't always happen but it could, though usually not with mothers that were already other-worldly.

He was doing a good job of distracting himself but she started to come, her walls dragging at him, gripping him tighter and milking him as she gave herself up to the abyss that engulfed her. He watched her through his orgasm, engulfed in his own pleasure but somehow lost in hers more. A slight shimmer, light blue, buzzed around her body, flexed and pulsed over him, her mouth an open "o" of wonder. She was the most beautiful thing he'd ever seen in his life. And she was his.

"Mesha?" he asked when her breathing returned to normal.

"Yes, baby?" She was sleepy. If he'd just be quiet for a minute.

"I don't know if Cade will allow it, but will you marry me? Before the baby's born?" He never thought he'd ask that question but with her it was easy, the right thing to do, the only thing he could do. He wanted her to be his wife.

"Sure, baby." She said it without consideration and he laughed. "Why are you laughing at me?"

"Are you sure you don't want to take some time to think about it?"

"Not at all. It's all I've wanted from the moment I met you, to always be with you. It doesn't take thinking about." She didn't mention that moment in the airport where she'd started to walk out of the airport but turned back.

"I've had a life. A very wicked life, I have to admit. There have been women, women I thought I loved, but they were just never right. None of them were worth telling my secret to. None of them loved me like you do."

His words trailed off and she thought he'd gone to sleep but he started to speak again.

"I never loved any of them the way I love you. It's not just the baby either. I love you. I love your curiosity, your strength, your fortitude. I love how funny you are, and how serious you are. I love how you want to find answers and seek them out. I just love you, Mesha." He squeezed her tight for a moment then let her go.

She rolled off him and looked over. "There's never been a man like you in my life, Kane. There's never been one that stuck around through the hard times, or been there when I needed them. You have been the only one. Loving you is hard, it's probably the hardest thing I've ever done. Trusting you was harder but I made the decision to do it. I can't let that go now. I can't let you. Whether Cade lets us marry or not, I'm yours and you are mine. For always."

She kissed him once more and got up. "Now get

some sleep, it's been a long day, night, day, night, whatever."

With a wiggle of her hips, she disappeared into the bathroom. Kane was asleep when she came out so she went downstairs, hungry once more. She was going to be huge if she kept eating like this. Annie was asleep on the couch and came in for her morning breakfast as Damesha prepared French toast.

Damesha knew life was going to change now, and not just because of the baby. Cade had accepted her into the clan. Maybe all of those strange noises would stop now. She'd long suspected Cade had something to do with it and thought she must be right even more now. Sitting at the table she started an email to Erika, telling her nothing about the last few days but warning her the baby might be premature. She didn't know how to explain a premature baby looking full term but knew something would reveal itself.

The most important bit of information she revealed was that Kane wanted to marry her. She knew this would send Erika into a frenzy of photographing wedding dresses in New York shop windows and would keep her busy. She was going to have to keep her friend busy over the next few weeks. This baby was growing quickly now and Damesha knew she might have weeks, or only days to go before it came.

There was too much to do, things they needed, and as Damesha ate her way through an entire loaf of sandwich bread cooked as French toast, she ordered things online. Her baby was going to have two parents. One might be a psychic and the other a shifter but she'd have two parents. Damesha wasn't exactly sure how she knew the baby was a girl but she knew the child had told her. One thing was for sure, the baby might not be a shifter but it was definitely psychic.

Damesha wasn't sure how she felt about passing the trait on to her child but knew it would never go through the torment she did. Her grandmother hadn't known any better. The woman who raised her thought she was doing what was best for her granddaughter. There had been no ill-intent or thoughts of abuse, her grandmother had simply been trying to spare her. But Kane said something about training, harnessing and control, she would want that for her baby as well. They were going to raise this kid right.

For a moment, Damesha wished Kane would get back in the truck and drive her to Texas again. Things had changed though, she didn't have to be afraid anymore. Cade was calming down and things were going to be different. A lot different, she thought as she considered the fact that vampires existed. People were psychics, shifters, she wondered if mummies and fairies were real too. Real fairies were said to be malicious little jokesters, not the beautiful little creatures that appeared in modern art now. No, Damesha was sure not all the creatures that inhabited the world were good. For now, she was happy with her man sleeping upstairs, her baby still tucked beneath her ribs, and a peaceful home. She wasn't going to start borrowing trouble, not when things were finally calming down.

Sighing with happiness Damesha went back to her laptop. It was time to get back to work, life was passing her by. She had a feeling life was about to turn upside down with this baby anyway. She couldn't wait.

A fire crackled in the fireplace, sending orange flames high and filling the room with heat that wasn't necessary. The flames soothed me though, soothed the ache between my shoulder blades and between my eyes. What the flames didn't soothe, a glass of bourbon eased away.

My brother Kane, always a loner, always defiant, had got his way. With a sigh I watched the flames, noting the way they jumped and danced around each other, almost erotic as they twisted together and became a new, bigger flame. Slamming the tumbler down on my desk in the dimly lit room, I cursed out loud. I was frustrated, I needed a woman.

I picked the glass back up after a moment; the contents danced in ambers swirls, and I took a swig. I knew a woman was the last thing I was going to get. Or needed really, just look at what had happened with Kane. We Alexanders weren't supposed to marry outside of our clan; it had been forbidden, though not written. Human mates could be turned into a shifter with a scratch or a bite and that was dangerous for all of us because we never knew how a human was going to react to becoming a shifter. With that came the danger of our secret being revealed. Then there was the danger of divorce. Divorces could turn ugly, secrets could be told, and our whole way of life, our lives, could be endangered.

No, it had always been the rule: never marry outside of the clan. Kane had broken that rule though, that tradition. Of course, Damesha was herself a magical, and she was soul-mated to Kane. That meant if she left Kane she committed suicide. Those that are soul-mated cannot be apart for long, as we all well knew. Death stalked separated soul-mates.

Sighing, I shifted in my chair, too tense to sit still. I had been against the union but now, I could see how Damesha had changed Kane, how she made him glow with happiness. An exception had been made, mainly because I was the leader of this clan and what I say goes. Some new blood might do us all some good anyway, I pondered as I thought about Kane and Damesha's child.

My niece. For a moment a smile played around my lips and I relaxed.

A knock came at my door and the urge to tell the knocker to fuck right off had to be bitten away. I was the leader of my clan, this was my job, even when it became too much of a burden.

"Hi there Cade, I've brought my niece to meet you. She's just finished college you know, and this is her first visit home since she left four years ago." A middle-aged woman bustled in, a tight white suit outlining her figure perfectly but doing little to attract my attention. Her white hair was perfectly coiffed and her makeup flawless. Her eyes revealed the lie her image created.

Greed rested in her brown orbs, avarice, a longing for more power that did little to make me want to look at her niece. I needed a bride, my clan kept insisting on it, kept bringing me candidates, and this one was only the latest.

I didn't want to deal with this, but it was my duty, I reminded myself for the millionth time that day. I had to provide the clan with an heir; I had to provide a new shifter to maintain our population, our status in the shifter world. I had to do all of this while I darted between endless meetings, settled countless disputes, and kept tabs on a group of shifters that wanted to cause trouble for the human and shifter worlds alike.

I finally looked at the young woman, admitting defeat. This was the only time I had to meet women, the only way I could think of to provide my clan with a wife they would approve. I felt my heart shrivel as I looked at the dyed black hair, overtanned skin, and too thick makeup of the young "farmgirl" before me.

She wore a tiny pair of denim shorts that showed off her long, shapely legs, shaved smooth and perfect. Her top was like something out of a costume store, a gingham number in blue and white checks, tied just above her belly button and left open with a tiny white top beneath to protect her modesty. She gave me a perfectly composed shy grin, filled with straight white teeth, her own brown eyes looking up at me from her under her lashes. Also, perfectly executed.

The only sign that I was bored was a slight tilt to my right eyebrow. Another perfect, fresh from the farm breeder with perfect hips and a beautiful face.

"No." I saw the girl's face crumple, she couldn't have been any more than twenty-one, and didn't care. Her aunt was offering her up for her own gains, and the poor girl probably had no idea what she was being led into. That or she craved the position as much as her aunt did. That's all any of the women from the clan wanted, it would seem; my money, my name, and my position. Too bad I didn't want any of them.

For a moment I felt an unfamiliar emotion, something I hadn't felt since I was a child, something I hadn't felt since my parents died and left me in charge of my brothers and my clan. I think it might have been anger, or hurt, perhaps even resentment. I wasn't sure and paused to examine it as the aunt ushered her now sobbing niece out, shooting me an angry glare.

"You'll have to choose sometime, Cade. We demand an heir!" Her words were loud and rude in the quiet setting but I didn't hear them, I was too busy examining this unfamiliar emotion.

I realized, after another sip of bourbon, that it was a mixture of all those emotions. These people trotting their offerings in here to me were making me feel like nothing more than a slab of meat, probably something all of these young women felt. I hated that feeling, even more than I hated feeling powerless to make my own decisions sometimes. As a clan leader, I had to think for everyone, not just myself.

Sometimes that got to me but I'd never let anyone know that.

This was my burden and my burden alone to bear. I would love to have a companion, the classical idea of a bride that would be my love, my best friend, and my partner in all things, but that was not going to be my fate. I could choose my bride though, whether she was a shifter or not. I did not have to provide them with a shifter bride; it was expected but not a written requirement.

There was the tradition to consider, the unwritten rule, but Kane had already broken it. And, I'm the leader, fuck the rules! If I have to marry, if I have to prove I'm a man by giving these people a bride, I'll find my own. From the looks of it, Kane is going to provide us with as many heirs as we need anyway, I might as well solve this problem the best way I know how to. Calling somebody else to sort it.

I remembered the website of a woman I knew in Florida. A woman that ran a high-class escort service for well-to-do clients who knew how to keep their mouths shut. She also offered another kind of service, mail order brides. Scratching at my tired jaw, I thought about the option. A mail order bride might be just what I need.

I scoffed at the old-fashioned name, but when it comes down to it, that's what the service was. I opened my laptop and found the site the woman kept, hidden behind firewalls, login screens, and other devices, and accessed the bride section. I knew the backgrounds of the women weren't the most spotless but these were all classy ladies, the best money could provide, and one of these would do for my needs.

At this point, all I wanted was a wife, one that could

be presented before my clan without a qualm, one that would always shine at my side, and one that didn't want anything but the security of my name and my money for the rest of her life. Open honesty was the only thing I craved, the only thing I truly wanted out of this newest demand of my clan.

I didn't want some young, nubile girl that wanted to lord it over her friends that she married the Alpha, or to be a feather in some aunt's cap, I didn't want an untried virgin who made social gaffs at every turn, or a wife that pretended to love me. I wanted a down to earth woman, one who knew the score from day one, and accepted me on the terms I'd set.

I scrolled through several pages, not finding a single profile that interested me until ice blond hair and an even icier blue gaze caught my eye. My lips parted as I looked at the woman, her gaze drawing me in. There was daring there, self-assurance, and something I don't quite think she knew she revealed. A vulnerability hovered around her lips, lips I wanted to reach out and touch. Were they as soft as they appeared to be? Or would they be frozen and hard, matching the appearance I saw right through?

This was a woman that knew how to deal with life, this was a woman that would know me for what I was, and take what I offered without question. She knew the realities of life and how to hide her true thoughts well. Except from experts like me who knew what to look for, because I'd lived the same kind of life.

I dug through her profile a little more and decided to call the woman that could make this happen. Jacqui, the name of the woman I had my eye on, was not the kind you approached without a battle plan, not from what I could tell about her from her profile. This would take some doing.

"Cade, I didn't expect to hear from you." The soft southern twang on the other end of the line let me know I'd reached Evelyn directly.

"No, ever since I've started this bride hunt I haven't had much time." I knew the sigh went all the way to the other end of the line but Evelyn was the kind of woman that I knew I could be softer around. She just drug it out of you without even trying.

"Not going well is it?" I couldn't tell if she was amused or considerate with that response.

"Not at all. Listen, I was going through the list of your ladies that want to find husbands and, well…" I let the words trail off, a moment of embarrassment taking over. I am Cade Alexander; I shouldn't be having to order a bride!

"Oh, darling, good! Let me see if I can guess which one caught your eye. Let me think." I could hear a manicured nail tapping against the older woman's teeth and smiled. It was a peculiar but endearing habit.

"Hmmm, you always ask for the more refined of my ladies when you visit Florida. Someone sophisticated and knows how to, ahem, *perform* her job well. You always go for dark-haired women as well. Now let me think."

I chuckled as she spoke, taking a sip of my bourbon as she thought on the other end of the line. And then she said a name and I knew she'd come to know me better than I thought she had.

"Jacqui Evans!" She sounded convinced she was right, and I knew my response wasn't needed but still, I garbled out one anyway.

"How did you know?" I couldn't fathom how she'd known Jacqui was the woman I was calling about.

"Cade, my darling, you're a man, you're all open books once you know what to look for!" Evelyn sounded rather smug and I was glad she couldn't see my moment of pouting, my bottom lip sticking out a bit as I frowned. Only she could produce that response in me.

"Well, that still doesn't explain it!"

"Alright Cade, calm down. Look, Jacqui is beautiful, she's around the right age for you, and she's the exact opposite of what you look for in a woman you just want to have some fun with."

"Right, but that *still* doesn't explain it!"

"Of course it doesn't, you're a man. It's like this, Cade, men don't pick the women they want to play house with the same way they pick bed partners. That goes especially for you. You are a powerful man, you need a jewel on your arm, not candy."

"Okay, that makes more sense." I was getting frustrated but I didn't want her to know that.

"And you called me. Any man with a lick of sense would know they need a plan to win Jacqui over. If you simply wanted to arrange a wedding with one of my girls you, Cade, would have handled it. Only a special case would get you to call me. That special case is Jacqui." She sounded tickled with her own deduction and I frowned some more, not sure I was enjoying her amusement as much as she was.

"Good work, Sherlock! Now, what do I need to do? As you said, not just anyone is going to win this woman. Tell me what I need to do." I poured another shot of bourbon in my glass and settled back into my leather desk chair. This might take a while.

"Well, you have to let her come to you. She's already asked to get out of the game we're in so I think I know just what to do."

"What's that? How is she supposed to come to me? I don't have a profile on that thing, website, whatever!" I wanted to growl, my shifter side getting a little annoyed now. I squashed it down, as in control of that as I was of everything else.

"I'll arrange everything, Cade. You just let me handle this, my darling. But, once she's on the hook, it's up to you to land her. Understand me? Jacqui is a special one, very special, and I won't force her to choose you. I think you two are suitable, and you have a lot in common. More than you realize, I'd say." Her words trailed off and my interest was piqued, but she started to talk again. "Now, listen, you let me handle this part, Cade, you'll hear from her soon enough. Don't let me down, alright?"

"I'll do my best, Evelyn. It's all I do. Ever."

We exchanged a few more pleasantries and then the line went dead. Evelyn was off to work her magic. I inhaled deeply as I pulled up the pictures of Jacqui one more time. The hardest part about this marriage, if it happened, was going to be keeping my hands off of her.

Jacqui was beautiful, seductive, but screamed don't touch me. That made me want to touch her, to comfort her, even more. A deep ache started in my groin as I looked at her but I couldn't allow it to blossom into anything more. I needed a wife in nothing more than name only, she wanted a husband that asked for a sexless marriage, with little contact. Maybe we were going to be perfect for each other.

As the ache in my groin continued to blossom, despite my efforts to squash it, I stood up and left the house. Removing my clothes, I shifted into the form of a black wolf, needing the exercise to take the edge off. I'll need to get this under control, and quickly.

I'd figure out the rest, such as not producing an heir, later.

Problem one had been solved. Maybe that was enough to stop the rumors that had started all of this in the first place. With the wind in my fur and my paws eating up the ground, I ran at full tilt, losing myself for the moment in not worrying, and just running.

ABOUT THE AUTHOR

Selina Coffey is a romance writer who lives happily in London with her husband and son. She is a hopeless romantic who grew up always believing in love and she is not ashamed to admit this! It is this belief that makes her so passionate about writing crazy love stories.

A stereotypical girly girl, she loves shopping. So whenever she gets a chance and the spare cash, you will probably find her browsing online for the next pair of shoes to add to her collection!

You can find her online at
www.selinacoffey.com

Contact her at
hello@selinacoffey.com